MY TOTEM CAME CALLING

Blessing Musariri & Thorsten Nesch

MAWEN𝖅I
HOUSE

We acknowledge the support of the Canada Council for the Arts for our publishing program. We also acknowledge support from the Government of Ontario through the Ontario Arts Council.

Cover design by Sabrina Pignataro

Cover photo: berry2046/Painting hand drawn animal multicolor zebra on a white background/Shutterstock

Blessing Musariri photo credit: Nyadzombe Nyampenza

Library and Archives Canada Cataloguing in Publication

Title: My totem came calling / Blessing Musariri & Thorsten Nesch.

Names: Musariri, Blessing, 1973- author. | Nesch, Thorsten, 1968- author.

Identifiers: Canadiana (print) 20190136464 | Canadiana (ebook) 20190136502 | ISBN 9781988449753 (softcover) | ISBN 9781988449760 (HTML) | ISBN 9781988449845 (PDF)

Classification: LCC PZ7.1.M87 My 2019 | DDC 823/.92—dc23

Printed and bound in Canada by Coach House Printing

Mawenzi House Publishers Ltd.
39 Woburn Avenue (B)
Toronto, Ontario M5M 1K5
Canada

www.mawenzihouse.com

CONTENTS

THE ZEBRA IN MY GARDEN

Through the bars of my window I see the zebra standing in the garden, beside the old jacaranda tree with its crooked branches and tiny green leaves. I know it's waiting for me, but nobody else can see it. Not Lameck, our gardener, who is now watering the border hedge—it's the kind of useless thing he does—and not anybody else. The other day when I saw the zebra in the middle of an intersection at rush hour, nobody in the street saw it, nor did any of the people at Sam Levy's shopping village. It's getting scary. And the zebra seems to pop up more and more often.

Maybe if I touch it, that would break the spell. This idea propels me off my bed. Landing with a thud on the hardwood floor, I run out of my room, startling our housemaid Nora, who stops what she is doing, dusting the expensive Chinese vase John brought home from a business trip last year, and gapes at me. I run down the hallway straight to the living room windows to check if the zebra is still there. It is, and I burst out of the open door into the garden. The grass is cool and soft under my feet and the afternoon heat warms my face as I race towards my hallucination.

Lameck swings around and stares as I run towards the

1

tree, my arms stretched out, ready to touch the zebra. But the closer I get to the animal, the more it fades away, and it disappears just as I reach it.

Panting heavily, I look around. Yes, I saw it disappear, but who knows, maybe it's hiding somewhere. Nothing makes sense about it, so anything is possible. Exhausted, I drop to the ground. I give up. It's official, I'm losing it. I'm going crazy. Not only am I forgetting stuff ever since I had the blackout and woke up in hospital, but now this zebra hunts me down. I saw it for the first time four weeks ago, when I woke up in the hospital room. It disappeared immediately when I blinked, and I thought the meds were screwing with my mind. But the second time followed soon after: it was in town, at the shopping centre.

"Hey Chanda. What are you doing?" Lameck jolts me from my daydream. Nora is peering through the open door, minding everyone else's business as usual.

"Nothing. I'm fine."

"Why were you running like that?"

"I . . . was running away from a bee."

He looks to Nora then back to me. "Is it gone? Did it sting you?"

"Yes, it's gone. It didn't sting me." I pretend to check my arms.

I can tell he wants me to say more, but I'm not in the mood. I get up, brush the dust off my legs, and walk back to the house. At the door I pause and turn around. No zebra, it's gone. Who knows for how long? Lameck points the hose at the bed of morning glories, this time watering something that actually needs it.

And why was I standing on my bed looking into the garden?

I have to talk to somebody about the zebra. So far I've kept its arrival in my life to myself, finding any possible excuse—the heat, the meds, some odd eyeball malfunction—to explain it. Lying to myself.

I should tell Rumbi and John—more respectfully, Mama and Baba, my parents. They're already worked up about my blackout and stuff, and the doctors having no clue what's wrong. Lameck or Nora will probably tell them about me running through the garden like some lobotomized boy band groupie. I have a feeling they didn't buy my bee story. I'd better be the one to tell the parents. I have to tell someone anyway, otherwise I'm just going to implode.

◆ ◆ ◆

I march into the living room, absent-mindedly scratching my hair, forgetting that I was at the hairdresser only yesterday and shouldn't ruin my Brazilian weave, but it itches like crazy. Rumbi and John are sitting next to each other on the couch. It's a weekday and very rare for John to be at home in the afternoon. He's been working from home more since my blackout, but it seems he's given himself a break at the moment, and they're watching one of those unbearable Nollywood dramas with a lot of weeping, wailing, and loud praying overcoming evil.

Rumbi gives me the look. I see that she's already braced herself for a calamity. She's been a bit of a nervous wreck since all this started.

"I need to talk to you, but you must promise you're not

going to overreact," I begin.

They look at each other in silent consultation, and then, as if reaching some telepathic conclusion, they both turn towards me. Rumbi carefully puts down the bowl of roasted peanuts they'd been sharing.

I don't know where to start, and I search for the right words.

"Are you pregnant?" John asks finally. I want to laugh. It's like we're all losing it in this house. Failing other explanations, my memory problem and strange behaviour can only mean one thing to him: his absolute worst nightmare—his only daughter, young and unmarried, knocked up by some halfwit party animal.

I can lose my memory, my mind, not recognize him, forget my own name, and all would be God's way, but baking a bun in my oven would be my own fault—and therefore his failing. Go figure.

"No, I'm not pregnant, Baba, so just relax yourself."

I'm being cheeky, but these days I can get away with a lot. The two Nigerian actresses they're watching on telly look half my age and are wearing a quarter of what I have to wear to pass John and Rumbi's fashion checkpoint on Friday nights. But on TV that's okay.

"What then?"

"I saw a zebra in our garden." No other way but just to say it.

John gets up and strides to the window. Each step he takes oozes his frustration—with me and my condition.

"A zebra! In our garden?"

"It was standing by the jacaranda tree."

John spins around to look at Rumbi.

"A zebra in our garden," he says to her, as if maybe she hadn't heard. "A zebra," he says again and laughs, shaking his head. He looks at Rumbi again and they do that telepathic thing. And I'm beginning to hate it. Rumbi gets up and goes to the window. They both stare at the garden. Of course they see nothing. Artificial giggling from the girls on TV.

"There is no zebra in the garden," John says.

"Yes, I know, it disappeared when I tried to touch it."

Rumbi returns to her seat.

"You saw a zebra in our garden this afternoon, and when you tried to touch it, it disappeared?"

"Correct."

Rumbi takes a sip of her Mazowe orange crush.

"A zebra," my father says again and turns off the Nigerian acting Olympics.

"Yes!" I slap the sides of my thighs for emphasis. "And not only there, in our garden, I've seen it now six or seven times . . . "

"The same zebra?"

"We didn't make introductions. But yes, I guess so."

"Where else did you see it? When, first?"

I'm standing still, on edge, as if the whole house could tip over the moment I move a centimetre. "First time at the hospital, then in the streets, in . . . "

Rumbi sighs, covering her mouth with a hand.

"Did it . . . move, did it do anything?" asks my father.

"No, nothing, just stood there, didn't move, not a bit."

"Did other people see it?"

"I haven't talked to anybody about it yet, but I'm sure

there would have been commotion in the shopping village if people had seen a zebra in front of Food Lover's Market."

John shakes his head in disbelief, mumbling a short prayer to the Lord.

Lameck knocks on the door frame.

John waves him off. "Not now! Go!"

Lameck knows what's good for him, so he goes away quietly.

Rumbi says, "I think we should take you to emergency."

"No!"

"Yes!"

"Why?"

"First, the thing with your memory, now a zebra . . ."

"It's not here anymore, nobody can see it but me. What are they going to do at the ER? Give me a tranquilizer so I can shoot it and bring it in?"

"Don't be so . . ."

"What?"

"You have to talk to a specialist."

"No, not another doctor. They only Xerox my brain until I have only black-and-white vision left!"

They have schlepped me to so many docs, making me sit in waiting rooms that smell of tears and worries, it took me days to get that stench out of my nose.

John says, "We should go with you to Cape Town. There is a centre for . . ."

"I'm not going."

"You must," Rumbi says.

"No. I'm. Not. Going!" I take a step back—and the house doesn't tip or shake a bit.

John gets up from the sofa. "Yes," he says firmly.

"Baba, give me some time, please, I don't want to go to any centre for anything."

Any other time I would be jumping for joy to go to Cape Town. This time, however, I have the feeling I won't return to Harare if I go.

"Okay then, but . . . " He has his hands on his hips and has his okay-I'll-give-you-one-last-chance look. "What do you suggest?"

"I . . . don't know."

He plays with his wedding ring. "Well, if you see the zebra again, we are going to Cape Town and that's that."

Phew. Bought some time, but I don't know how much. I won the fight but not the war.

"I think this calls for prayers. Let's pray together," my father says.

Crap! Should have made a clean getaway while the going was good.

I really wish John and Rumbi hadn't decided to be born again. It has added another level of complication to our already stressed relationship. We kneel down on the carpet, close our eyes, fold our hands. Anything is better than doing the hospital run, so we pray and I say Amen the loudest.

◆ ◆ ◆

My aunt, Tete Frasia, lives in an apartment in a brand-new building on the corner of Seventh Avenue and Baines, with a balcony overlooking Greenwood Park. John bought it for her out of gratitude. She was a big help at the beginning of his career before he hit it big. And I have to admit, he doesn't forget those who support him. She moved into the building a couple of years ago, after leaving her husband who had taken to using her as a punching bag. She had had enough when he pushed her and she fell on the stone veranda at a friend's house and injured her hip.

As I arrive I see her unpacked boxes languishing in the corners. The only effort she's made to settle down here is to put up the faded photographs of her parents and a painting of a landscape in the village where she and John grew up. I once asked her about it, and she said that one day I would go there and see it for myself.

Tete Frasia is the only one of John's relatives whom he's tolerated after he became a Pentecostal sheep—as she puts it. He says everyone else is too caught up in ancestor worship and the old, cursed, unchristian ways. Both my grandparents—his mum and dad—are no longer on this side of the world, and as the head of the family he is less tolerant. He routinely banishes from his life anybody who refuses to leave those old beliefs where they belong, in the past.

Tete Frasia stands very straight and her face is still smooth, although here and there she has dark spots, as if she's been burnt by the sun. I'm always telling her to wear a hat when she is out. When she was with her husband, she wore long pleated skirts, plain white blouses, and a headscarf. These days she goes to the salon down the road and has them put big curlers in her hair, which is almost all white but thick and falls down to her shoulders. She even wears a dab of brownish-red lipstick every now and then and—occasionally—blue jeans! The first time I saw her in them I was totally sparked. What has always fascinated me about Tete Frasia are the brass and copper bangles around her wrists and a pair of earrings that sit on her earlobes like silver and copper beetles. As a child, I always felt there was something magical about them, and about her. I have never seen her without those earrings.

Her big thing is Zumbani tea. She drinks it like there's no tomorrow, says it's the best medicine in the world, for the body and the soul. There is always hot tea in her house ready for guests, although I am the one she mostly sees. And now we are sitting in her small, rather dim, and often too-cold dining area, on dark wooden chairs that seem too big for us, at a round table big enough for eight people. After the usual greeting from me, and her reply, "I'm well, though the tooth of time gnaws on me," followed by an awkward silence bridged by sips of tea, she asks, "Is all well where you are coming from?"

It always seems to me that Tete Frasia senses what I'm about to say before I even open my mouth. Of course, she knows this is not my usual bimonthly visit—which is not due until next Saturday. I know that if anyone will understand what is happening to me, it will be Tete Frasia, but I'm not sure where to start. Nothing seems to ever strike her as too fanciful or out of the norm, so I decide to jump right in, but I keep my gaze focused on my fingernail tracing a flower pattern on the tablecloth. It's quiet outside, there is only the noise of birds and the cars on Herbert Chitepo Avenue in the distance. I take a deep breath.

"Tete, yesterday . . . and a few times before . . . I saw . . . uhm . . . a zebra."

Out of the corners of my eyes I see her eyebrows lifting. Then she hums a tune that could mean anything and picks up her cup with both hands.

After a long sip she says, "What did the zebra do?"

As I expected, she is not fazed. She is awesome like that. I should have just come straight to her instead of telling Rumbi and John, who are so freaked out by anything that comes out of my mouth.

"Nothing, it just stood there."

"A zebra?"

"Yes."

"Hmmm!"

She gets up from the table and comes back with a plate of scones that had been cooling on the island between the small kitchen and the dining area. She balances a scone on the lip of my tea saucer and sits back to take another sip of her tea.

"It didn't move at all?" she asks, finally.

"No."

Another tea-sipping break. Outside, a crow lands on the balcony and caws loudly as if to contribute to the conversation.

"Did you tell your parents?"

"Yes, wasn't a good idea."

"Why? What did they say?"

"I barely avoided being put on the plane to see the next expert. But they said if I see it again, we're going to Cape Town without delay."

"So, will you tell them when the zebra appears again?"

"I wasn't planning to."

Tete Frasia raises a hand and says, "Promise me, you will tell them next time the zebra visits you."

"I . . . " Eish, I don't want to promise anything, and *visits* me? More like *torments* me again.

"Promise!"

"Ag, Tete . . . okaaay, I promise."

With a grunt she pulls herself up, goes over to the stove and brings the teapot to the table. She tops up my cup and refills hers. Then she places the pot on the woven mat between us as her bangles clink softly at her wrists. I realize that this is the sound I have come to associate with being in her house drinking tea—the soft clinking music of metal against metal, a sound of reassurance, because whenever I fail to get through to Rumbi and John, Tete is my refuge and my helper.

She sighs as she sits down again.

I take a sip of tea.

"So what do you think you should do?" she asks.

"What I should do?"

"Yes, if you don't want to see another shrink with your parents, what do you think of doing about this visitation?"

"I . . . I don't know. I hope the zebra doesn't come back."

"You really think it won't?"

"I hope . . . oh, Tete, please at least let me hope!"

She doesn't say anything.

Sometimes even her silences are riddles.

"Do you know anything about this zebra, Tete? Is it . . . I know that it's your totem, yours and Baba's, and also mine, I guess."

"What do you think?"

"Well, first I thought it was the meds, but I've stopped taking the pills. Could the scans have triggered the hallucinations, do you think?"

She doesn't respond, which is a clear no from her.

"Why then? What's happening to me? You know, don't you?"

I don't know how, but I know she knows. Carefully, she places her cup on the delicate saucer. Her favourite tea set is bone china acquired during the "liberation" war. She told me that when she started thinking about leaving her husband, this was the first thing she smuggled out of the house, one piece at a time in a small handbag. During their marriage, she had to feign indifference to it, because he smashed everything else she loved. Right now, she is tracing the gold filigree on the saucer as if in a kind of trance.

"Our people used to see these kinds of things in the old days, before . . . all these machines and medicines."

"Saw what?"

"Their totem spirits. Life was very different then. We did things differently."

"And?"

She sips her tea, so do I. Tea in Tete's home is a ritual of conversation.

"I don't know," she says.

"You . . . must know . . . something."

"For each person it is different." She weighs her words the way she weighs out her tea leaves as she spoons them into the pot.

"Oh, that's just great."

"Maybe you should go to Gumindoga."

"Me?"

"Yes."

"Gumindoga? What for?"

"Maybe there is somebody at that place who saw it too. Maybe they can tell you more."

Now I am the one who needs to weigh my words. Gumindoga, our ancestral village, is so far away and so remote that I hardly ever think about it. I last went there with Rumbi and John before I started school. It's nothing but rocks and bushes and old people in mud huts with straw roofs.

"That's like sixteen hours away!"

"Five," she says, with a laugh and a look in her eyes that could mean, What a silly girl you are! "If I could still drive . . . ," she continues, rubbing her hip gingerly, "I would take you. I wish I could."

"Yeah, but why would I be going to Gumindoga, Tete? Apart from maybe meeting someone who is also seeing this zebra, is there actually a real, definite reason I should go?"

You are in an odd state of limbo when medical experts give up on you one by one and nobody can tell you how your condition will change in the future, for better or for worse. To be honest, I feel that it is not something that doctors want to really understand. If they cannot find it in their textbooks, they pass it on to the head people. I'm not crazy. This I know. Tete Frasia knows it too, she's just being coy about it. Usually she can't stop telling me what to do.

"There are people there who know things. They have answers to questions we don't know how to ask, old medicine. We wouldn't be around if they never had cures, you know. Most new pills are made out of herbs we've used for hundreds of years."

"Yeah, but . . . "

"And the spirits—people in the rural areas are still connected with their world."

Yeah! Tell me about it! I've always approved when John refuses to entertain our rellies from upcountry. Even I sometimes pick up the weird energies flying off them. Anyway, I don't know where this conversation is going.

"Their ancestor spirits, their totems," Tete continues, attempting to explain.

"But I have no connection to them!"

"Maybe you have more connection than you think."

How can I gently tell her, "hell no," without insulting her? Ah, yes, "Mama and Baba would never allow it." I am careful not to abuse their first names in Tete's presence, I don't need a scolding on top of everything.

"What makes you so sure?"

"Please." I mimic the singing in father's church. In this at least, I have Tete on my side. We're both agreed that working your butt off all week, only to give a percentage of your paycheque to a religious spin doctor in a fancy suit on Sundays, is three slices short of a loaf. They are alleluia-crazy.

"You shouldn't do that!" she says, smiling behind her cup.

"Tete, why isn't life easier?" I look into my cup. The tea is finished.

"Because it is called life, which has its ups and downs."

"I'm pretty down."

"How is your friend?"

It's so funny. There's a way all tetes say "friend," meaning boyfriend and not any other friend. It must be some secret linguistic skill they are born with as paternal aunts.

"Fine."

"Your friendship?"

"Everything is okay. Actually he is more understanding about the whole situation than I expected."

"Really? A boy, that's rare."

We laugh and she laughs so hard she holds her chest. Then she stops and pulls out one of the three necklaces she's wearing and places it on the table before me. "Here."

A piece of red brown stone in what I fancy as the shape of Africa lies before me.

"That is yours," I say.

"Just in case."

"What case?"

"In case you do go."

"Where?"

"To Gumindoga."

"No." I slide it back to her.

She insists, opening my hand with her crumply soft fingers, always colder than mine, and places it into my hand, which she closes into a fist. "I myself won't go anymore . . . "

"Don't say that."

"It belongs there."

"But not me."

"Maybe one day."

"Tete."

"Ah," she plays her last trump card, a finger raised, "Would you refuse a gift from me? Your elder, your beloved aunt?"

"Okay, Tete."

She smiles. I put the necklace around my neck.

◆ ◆ ◆

My eyelids are shut tight. By day Harare is always buzzing, Combi touts calling out their destination, cars speeding on the highway, the siren of an ambulance or the presidential motorcade—especially along the Borrowdale Road; but at night, it's quieter and the sounds are far away. The neighbourhood dogs stop barking, and our house is conducting its symphony of settling-down sounds. I should be deep in sleep, but my breath is racing and my pulse won't stop. I squeeze a glance through my fluttering eyelids. It's standing in front of my bed, in the light of the moon shining through the barred window, one short metre away from my feet. The zebra.

It doesn't move, just stares at me like a stuffed animal of some trophy hunter. But I'm mentally prepared this time, even though it's still freaking weird to see it at four a.m. in my room. My pocket vidcam is on the bedside table next to my iPhone. Without a sound my arm slithers out of the sheets. I grab the camera and turn it on like a ninja. If I film the zebra, it was there.

I check the finder, point the lens at the spot where the zebra is standing. I see nothing in the finder. Lowering the vidcam, I blink and open my eyes wide. The zebra is there, before me, gawking at me from the middle of the room. Quickly I press the record button on the cam. I rewind and take a look: there is nothing on my short movie, not a shadow, no pixelation, absolutely nothing. I put the cam down on the mattress. A real *Twilight Zone* moment.

I am alone with my zebra that doesn't want to leave and I can't prove its existence to anyone else. What now? This sucks donkeys' balls, as the boys would say in *South Park*. I am this close to just screaming, screaming in frustration. If I scream, the rest of tonight will involve an ambulance and an emergency room visit followed by a red-eye flight to Cape Town, first class.

Maybe I could jump and try to touch it. I would probably just hurt myself and put myself back in the ambulance-emergency room Cape Town scenario. Maybe I should just tell it to go; sometimes it's the simplest solutions that work. Why haven't I thought of this before?

I gather my guts, take a deep breath, and say very firmly, "Leave! Shoo, go away."

It doesn't listen—in fact, it shows no reaction at all, and I realize that not only am I having a recurring hallucination, I am now talking to it. I'm going cuckoo. My parents think so anyway, they're just waiting for the slightest reason to ship me off to the loony bin.

None of the supposedly great doctors I've seen know what's wrong with me. I keep forgetting chunks of my life, randomly, what yesterday morning or in the afternoon, the day before, last week, sometimes half an hour ago, sometimes half a day; an inexplicable short-term memory loss that pops up in my reality, leaving it with holes and tunnels like Swiss cheese. The doctors were totally X-ray happy, scanning my skull in every possible way, putting electrodes on my temples, and running every other test in the world, because my parents can afford them. But they all came to the same conclusion: I am healthy. One guy even suggested that I—"a beautiful young lady" actively pursuing a career in the TV business—was faking the whole thing to get attention and airtime on some talk show. As if!

You see, the good stuff I seem to forget, crap like that festers in my brain. That quack I'd like to forget.

But never mind all that, my zebra is still watching me. What if it doesn't disappear? I'll have this constant friend I don't want always by my side.

I'm fighting tears. What do I do now? All I know is that waking my parents and telling them is not an option.

◆◆◆

I can't tell Tete Frasia either, I promised her I would tell Rumbi and John, but that's a no-go. My two besties, Nomsa and Samu, are more my frenemies at the moment. They are quite likely to start channeling CNN news and spreading my new talent for zebra-spotting across Harare; or to print T-shirts showing me with a bedsheet pulled up to the nose and a caption saying, "I see zebras." They were both kind of strange to me after I came back from the hospital, not sure how to deal with my condition. This is when you know who your true friends are and it seems I'm in a bit of a deficit right now. The only person I can talk to about this condition of mine is Swagga.

And this here tonight needs my boy Swagga, he's always got my back. Without taking my eyes off the zebra, I reach for my phone, absently thinking, maybe I should give him a name, maybe it's a she. Ag! This is really dire. Swagga's cell rings six times before he takes the call. "This had better be a deep gwaan shawty. It's the middle of the night!"

"It's morning. Other people are already up, catching Combis to go to work." With the back of my hands I wipe my cheeks dry. I don't want him to know I've been crying. It's weird, I don't like to appear weak around Swagga.

While I was doing my internship at ZTV during our August hols, Swagga was helping out at his father's law office whenever he was needed—which was almost never. He's just that kind of guy—not serious.

"Speak now or forever hold your peace." Swagga sounds like he's been out on a bender, pretending to be the tough guy even at four a.m. I'm sure his eyes are sealed shut and he's been pissing Grey Goose all night.

"I need us to make like Dora and go on an adventure. Rumbi and John have me on lock-down. They want to take me for psyche evaluation. You know I'm not crazy."

"Dude, if Rumbi and John heard you calling them by their first names, they would blow a gasket. Honour thy mother and father, you heathen child."

This is classic Swagga. Lack of focus. We met at school during sports. He was hiding behind the pavilion to avoid cross-country. Not that he is in a bad shape, not at all, he is very sporty and has a beautiful body, well trained. He just wanted to show off how smart he was, outwitting the sports teacher. And he managed to do just that—even scoring an A on his report card, for effort. Some people have it all. Me too, until four weeks ago.

"Hey . . . ," he starts.

"Listen to what I'm saying bruh, I need to break out of Chirkurubi prison, so come and get me in thirty minutes, and pack an overnight bag, if you want."

"By overnight bag, you mean Mr Condom?"

"Ha! Ha! You got jokes! Just come and get me."

"Yeah babe."

"Swagga." I look out of the window and see half of a full moon, the other half is hidden behind the big avocado tree.

"What's up, babe?"

"I'm not going deep into this right now, but you know my gwaan with the memory issues—you know what I am talking about. I have to solve it myself, and I'm thinking I should go right back to the roots."

"Roots? Like in . . . "

"Just come! I need to go somewhere, I'll tell you everything when you get here and you can go back or stay with me."

When I turn my head back straight, the zebra is gone. As if it had never been there. Mountains of rocks are falling off my shoulders, I had really feared it was here to stay this time.

"Chanda?"

"What?"

"Where do you . . . ?"

"Dude! Just come. Now. Okay?"

"I guess."

"You guess?"

A crackling in the phone. Is he covering the phone with his hand?

"Swagga? Sw—"

"Yeah, yeah, on my way."

"Okay."

I don't want to wait until I can't remember his name, I

have to take action. I kiss him through the phone and end the call, hoping he doesn't go back to sleep.

I can count on Swagga, most of the time. After that first meeting behind the school pavilion, we became fast friends, and since we live in neighbouring suburbs, we started seeing a lot of each other outside of school as well. Whenever I don't feel like driving, or when my ride has been confiscated—like for the last four weeks now, thanks to my blackouts—I just holla and he swings by to get me. Usually. During daytime, of course. It was on one of these rides two years ago that he kissed me for the first time and asked me to be his girlfriend. It feels like an eternity. Along with my memory loss, I have a strangely altered perception of time, I can't remember whether things happened a long time ago or just now. It's like a camera lens moving in and out of focus and clicking on random images that aren't even located in the same place and trying to present it as a sequence. If there is nothing structurally wrong with me, then it's a mental thing. I am convinced I'm not going crazy, so that leaves one other possibility.

❖ ❖ ❖

It doesn't take me long to pack my stuff. I fly through the room like a whirlwind, suddenly all excited about the trip. Tete Frasia's stone around my neck feels clunky but right. I'll phone her in the morning when we're halfway and ask her for directions. I stop to write a note to Rumbi and John that I am fine but can't say where I'm going, just so they know that I haven't been abducted by aliens. I leave by the front door and tiptoe across the garden, avoiding the glaring moonlight. It's the first time I've felt wide awake and clear-headed in weeks, since I woke up in the hospital with visions of the zebra and began losing small segments of time. Everything I've done so far has been linked to my condition. I desperately want to change that and go back to normal.

Earlier, when Swagga said my name—Chanda—I had a strange feeling. Since my condition appeared, every time someone says my name I start to get anxious, I feel there's something I should be doing, only I don't know what. There are times when I think all this is John's fault. In a misguided sense of I don't know what—family loyalty or something—John named me after my great-grandmother, a woman who stubbornly refused to live up to the meaning of her name, Chandagwinyira, the one who perseveres. This great-grandmother of mine persevered at no kind of work that needed doing but would sit quietly in the sun all day. She saw everything that happened in the village and she never forgot. She caused plenty wahala, remembering too many things people wanted forgotten. Even as she lost her sight and the ability to move around unaided, she could identify to which branch of the family tree anyone belonged, and everything else about them, just by their voice.

Ironically enough, I am failing to live up to this particular talent. Not that I ever had a formidable memory, but I do have a penchant for wanting to document things on film, along the lines of reality shows. And so, in that way, I am a modern Ambuya Chandagwinyira Tiregeyi, never without my pocket-sized vidcam. Basically, my name came with an inheritance. I know it sounds really flimsy, but I am a great

22

believer in the theory that certain names come with certain character traits. Anyway, reaching the bottom of the garden, I climb over the wall. It is topped with razor wire, but there's a place in one corner where Swagga and I cut a hole the past New Year's Eve when I had to sneak out to go to a party at Platinum. It was way overgrown there and the wire was sagging so it was easy to cut and use the leaves and branches to hide our handiwork. Thank goodness Mukoma Lameck is a pretty indifferent gardener—out of sight, out of mind. This part of the garden is his blind spot.

Landing on the street side, I brush off the sand and cobweb from my legs and absently think to myself that I'm looking a bit thick in the thighs again. Nobody seems to have noticed, but maybe they are just being polite.

Hunkering down between two hibiscus bushes, I wait for Swagga. Life is funny—the thought comes—here I am sneaking out of my home to run away to a village I can barely remember. Me!—whose idea of slumming it is private boarding school or the driver's pickup truck on the days neither Rumbi nor John can pick me up from school. I am used to bright lights, big city, and being in the lime-light. I started off my Hollywood dream as a kiddies' TV presenter, but now I like to be behind the camera. So far, I've done my version of *Rich Kids of Beverly Hills* using my so-called besties and other frenemies from Borrowdale Brooke and sometimes Swagga. Five months ago, I decided to do a short doccie on life downtown for my film school application, and that's the last thing I remember about that. I woke up in the hospital not knowing how I got there. Something crunk must have gone down, but I just can't remember what. Sometimes I think I might just remember, but then that small thread disappears. It's frustrating.

I brush off some ants that seem to think my leg is part of their daily obstacle course, and I hiss, "Swagga, do hurry up." Squatting on the ground waiting for a ride to some long-forgotten place is not my idea of a happening time. There's still a bit of a chill left over from winter, but it's bearable with my light cardi. A branch cracks behind me and I hear Lameck's voice saying, "Chanda, what are you doing here? At this time?"

I need this encounter like I need a pimple on my nose.

"Eish, Mukoma! Are you trying to kill me, sneaking up on me like that? Never mind me, what are you doing here at this time?"

"I went to see my mother in Chitungwiza last night, and I didn't want to be late back to work so I got up early. Combis are a problem between six and eight and your father said if I am late one more time he will fire me. What about you? What's your story?"

I can tell by the way he is watching me very carefully that he thinks I'm having one of my episodes and he should be prepared to act quickly.

"Don't worry about me, Mukoma. I'm just . . . " I follow his gaze to my backpack, so I decide to tell him the truth. "I'm going on a trip."

"And you are waiting for the bus or a Combi down there?"

I get up. "No."

"So?"

"For a friend."

"This early?"

"Yes."

Clearly he knows there is more to it and he's dying to ask, but he understands the rules of this game. If it was something I wanted him to know, it wouldn't involve me crouching outside the garden wall at this time of morning. I see him weighing the likelihood of his being told the truth and deciding that it's just about zero. The dog next door starts barking as if there were no tomorrow. Stupid dog, almost got me busted New Year's Eve.

Mukoma Lameck is scratching his head, a look of consternation on his usually smiley face.

"Do your parents know about this?"

He is asking just out of courtesy, of course; he knows that if they knew I wouldn't be crouching in the bushes waiting for a ride. If I lie, he might get into trouble later for giving false information. He doesn't deserve that. He's worked here since I was a kid, and even though I diss him sometimes, he's more or less part of the family. John threatens to fire him on a regular basis, but he never does. It's just part of their repertoire, but this time it may well happen because of the seriousness of the situation. The barking stops. I tell him that no, they don't know.

Mukoma Lameck shakes his head. "Then I can't let that happen."

"Mukoma!"

"Come, go inside."

"No."

"Talk . . . Tell . . . Ask your parents first."

"Mukoma Lameck, please, why? You are never so early even."

"Unfortunately today. Now for the two of us, come."

"No!"

He grabs my arm. "I can't let that happen."

"Please, Mukoma."

"Ch . . . listen, you are young."

"Yes! And if I go back in there, they will take me to South Africa. They will keep me there, institutionalized, on drugs . . . "

"Cha . . . "

"Yes, like a veggie, and I will never get out again!"

"You're exaggerating. Your parents would never do such a thing."

I shake my head.

"They are doing all they can to help you."

"They think they are helping me, but they don't know what they're doing."

"Don't say that. Of course, they do."

"Mukoma . . . "

"Come now!"

I rip my arm free. "No way," I hiss. "And if you don't let me be, I'll just run."

"Where will you run, Chanda?"

"I'm not telling you. I'll run away and it will be your fault for not letting me go where I need to go."

"Now you are really being . . . " He stops himself just short of saying, "crazy." Yes, that word is under sanctions in our house now, it doesn't pass anybody's lips anymore.

He says, "Are you running away now?"

"No! Not if you just leave me here."

"Where are you going?"

"I can't tell you."

He's really torn, picturing himself out of a job, if John and Rumbi find out about our run-in here. Shame. Mukoma Lameck is generally a very honest man, even when he gets into trouble. It's like he can't help himself, his mouth opens and the truth comes out.

I tell him, "Don't worry about it Mukoma. I'll be fine."

"What if your parents ask me? If I saw you, or when did I see you last?"

It's going to be virtually impossible for him, but I try anyway. "Just forget you saw me."

He shakes his head. It's getting lighter and the dawn bird chorus has started in the branches above. They make quite a racket, and on the main road two houses down from us there is the increased sound of traffic. I wish I could fold my arms together and blink like the genie on TV to make Swagga appear this instant. It would be like a scene from an action film, Swagga pulling up with a screeching of wheels, doing a 360 while leaning over to open the passenger door and yelling, "Come on shawty, let's bounce!" Instead, there is the sound of Mukoma's palm rubbing his morning stubble, and about two gates down, the sound of a house alarm going off, like it always does, because the dad of that house always forgets to turn it off before opening the window.

It's getting crucial now.

Mukoma Lameck's eyes follow the twisted razor wire on the wall—there goes my escape route, I think.

"Please, Mukoma Lameck, for once in your life, just don't remember something. They probably won't even ask you, because I wrote them a note telling them where I'm going."

He looks doubtful. I grab his hand.

"I promise you."

Finally, he rolls his eyes and says, "Okay Chanda. If you promise me you told them, then I am trusting you. You know that I will be in big trouble if you are lying to me."

"Yes I know. I'm not lying."

He clears his throat and eases his hand out of mine. He's a little embarrassed by the contact. He says, "This time I'm going to fix that wire."

Now it's I who feel the heat rushing up all over the face. "What . . . how . . . You know about it?"

"Being quiet doesn't mean I'm stupid."

"And you didn't fix it?"

He shrugs his shoulders. "I wish I had, now."

"Thank you." I'm beginning to see him in a whole new light. Note to self: do not underestimate people.

Finally! The wheels of a car come crackling closer, no headlights on.

"My ride."

"Chanda, be careful," he says. I can tell he is having second thoughts already.

"I will be fine. I promise."

He turns away before the car arrives and I know he doesn't want to see any more that he might have to forget. I breathe a sigh of relief and pray that nobody else in our cul-de-sac has an early-rising gardener out and about. Danger—that stupid noisy dog—had better keep his trap shut!

◆ ◆ ◆

When the car pulls up, even more annoying than the fact that Swagga has brought along Jix is that they are in Jix's old yellow Citroën with boyfy riding shotgun. I mean, the car is not bad, but we're heading for the sticks here, and Swagga's baby Jeep would be far better suited, not to mention more comfortable. Instead of my—at least semi-imagined—romantic trip, we are passengers at Jix's mercy and emotions, and he can be quite a flip-flop.

The two of them have known each other since kindergarten, their time together interrupted by Jix's family's great idea to go away to London. The stay lasted about two years before they moved back to good old Harare, 'cause their dear son discovered Ecstasy at school, consuming and selling it and getting busted by police. When all other measures failed and because he was still a minor, the family struck a deal with Her Majesty's judiciary and were allowed to move back unscathed. He brags that he's not allowed to set foot on the Queen's soil as long as he lives.

"Hi," I say, and he "hi"s back and adds, "I brought my sleeping bag, too."

"Wohoo."

I lean in through the front passenger window and kiss Swagga, who doesn't even bother to remove his shades. It's going onto five now and getting light, so we need to hustle. I'm praying Mukoma Lameck doesn't change his mind and sell me out. At least Jix is good at undercover missions and didn't come roaring down the road, lights blazing and beats thumping. He's generally a shady type of guy, who can disappear in a crowd, even if that crowd consists of two people.

I open the door, throw my backpack in, and follow.

"Dude!" Swagga takes the word out of my mouth. He has known me long enough to know what I'm thinking. I don't even have to ask. It's one of two things: Swagga went out and lost the keys to his car—most likely scenario—or he pranged it. I'm hoping not, 'cause he's been "borrowing" his dad's Range when he's away.

It's neither.

"Sha, the cops impounded my spaceship!" he says.

This is a new one.

"They took your dad's ride? How come?"

"Eish! You know how these guys are. Asking me for this and that, just harassing me, you know."

"Were you dorped?"

"No, I was completely sober—it was just nine o'clock. I was on my way to get Jix. They just said, ah jack, go get the reg book for the car. They knew I didn't have the papers with me, so I called Jix to come get me and we went to the cabin, but we couldn't find the book—I reckon it's at the bhally's office or something. I wanted to get my car, but I couldn't find the keys and eish, it was just drama with my mom, so I decided to spend the night at Jix's. I didn't want to be around when the bhally comes home and hears about his car from the quan."

I get where he's coming from. Swagga's dad, his bhally, is just another kind of fish—sure he spoils Swagga, but eish! When he's angry he gets basic. Swagga's mom, aka the quan, the queen, doesn't even try anymore with her son, she just feeds him, makes sure he's dressed as decently as she can make him, and that he's going to school. She leaves the rest up to his dad.

We're still just parked outside my house.

"Let's get moving!" I yell.

"Well, it would help, your highness, if you would tell me where we're going," Jix says.

For a moment, I hesitate. Then I tell Jix to head for the Masvingo road, and I sit back and relax. For the first time since my big blackout I feel like my head is somewhat clearing up.

ON THE ROAD

After we leave the city centre behind us, and I've told them the true reason for this trip, I turn my camera on the passing view outside. Chivhu's first houses, cars on the road, and random people blur in my camera viewer into a horizontal waterfall of colours. Streaks of yellow, red, and blue. No zebra. I begin to think that if I never ever want to see it again, I may have to experience my life through a camera lens.

Chivhu Town Centre is a dustbowl full of people. I'm sure there's more to it, but I always think of these roadside towns as just that, roadside towns dotting wildernesses, and here and there the little villages slowly bleeding their small populations into Harare. It's so crowded in Harare these days, these people should be tested for some skill or level of education before they are allowed to come and stay, because honestly! Right now this place is just busy with people on the road, getting on and off buses, cars stopping at the service stations to refuel. We pass what was once a truly grand hotel, when as a kid I came this way with Rumbi and John. The boys in front are quiet, probably mulling over the zebra situation. Swagga has already planted doubts in me, saying he would like to see me surviving in the wild, his girl who loves her queen-size bed, Wi-Fi, long showers, and the newest movies on plasma TV.

Jix rolls down the window.

"Good idea," mumbles Swagga and does the same.

They are right, the sun is heating up the car and we don't have air con, but just as the windows are fully open the wind rips through my hair with gale force.

"Close it!" I yell.

"What? Why?" Jix meets my eyes in the rearview mirror.

"The wind is ruining my snip!" I say, holding my hair with both hands.

"So?"

"So, close the windows!"

"No way I'm driving the whole day with the windows closed!"

And Swagga says, "Babe, it's either that or die of heat exhaustion, you just have to live with it."

"Oh, thank you! This is the best Brazilian hair money can buy."

"Was," Jix drops.

By now I know I look like tumbleweed, I can feel dozens of invisible fingers massaging my head. So I give up my protest. One grand gone with the wind, I might as well have thrown the money off the top of Joina City. Whoever picked it up would have had better use of it. Going rural has meant ditching my comfort zone even earlier than I imagined.

Swagga was right, but his plasma TV remark was also to make fun of me. It feels like he does that more often lately,

I mean, after my blackout. My blackout is a time threshold. There's before and after my blackout. Eish.

But am I too much of a muSalad?

After this summer, Swagga will go to university. My party boy. He can't wait. I'm not sure I like that. I'll hardly see him, maybe every second break, or once a year. And I don't even know what I will be doing anyway. It's going to suck. I've been bracing myself for months now for that moment when we will go our different ways. Swagga wants to party all the time, get dorped, and dance. And then he attracts every skanky girl in the perimeter, like an electric flytrap. They only want to be around him 'cause he's like a drinks carousel when he goes out. His dad is a player and everyone knows it, but his mother acts like she doesn't and they both give Swagga everything he wants. He got into UCT—beats me, how—and doesn't know what he wants to study there, he just picked a course at random. He can be such a loser sometimes.

Does *nice* cut it for a solid relationship, though, can it survive like the crazy love, the one you would die for—or with, no matter what?

The waterfall of colours on my viewer becomes less blurry. We slow down, and I press STOP.

"What is it?" I ask.

Jix knocking on the steering wheel says, "I need to fill up with petrol one more time before we dive into the wilderness."

◆◆◆

We get out to stretch our legs and my bum is already numb

from the potholes we've bounced over, on shock absorbers built for the streets of Paris thirty years ago. Jix drives as if he's playing a video game, collecting points by hitting potholes. When one crack sent me airborne, I reached out to grab whatever I could and the nail on my index finger broke off. I've been rattled around on the bumpy road so much that if I was a cow I would be shitting butter.

"I'm missing your Range," I whisper to Swagga.

"Me too."

But Jix surprises me by filling a jerry can with emergency fuel. It's something I didn't even think about, and I am forming some respect for him. He seems more prepared for this longish road trip than either myself or Swagga, in fact he seems more organized altogether. I usually travel with Rumbi and John or the driver, and Swagga only ever leaves town when he has to go somewhere with his old man. Jix seems to have some interesting things in his boot.

I have about two hundred and fifty bucks on me, and I use some of it to stock up on a few snacky things—chocolates, biscuits, a six-pack of Coke and three bottles of water. Jix has brought a small cooler, and Swagga buys ice and a six-pack of Red Bull.

On the way back to the car, Swagga lopes in front of me—that's the only way I can describe the way he walks. He's tall and slim with jeans hanging as low as he can get them without them actually falling off. I think the only person he loves more than himself is the dude in the picture he has of himself. He's hooked his shades on the gold chain around his neck, and he chews away on a thick piece of game biltong. I don't think people eat zebra, but you never know.

They say you are not supposed to eat your totem, at least that's what Tete Frasia told me, so I've always just stuck to beef biltong. Swagga doesn't seem bothered about that. I guess it's because nobody here sells monkey meat, as far as I know.

Swagga and I put the food and drinks into the car. Tete Frasia's necklace is bobbing against my skin, he hasn't even noticed it. I mean, he didn't ask me where I got it from, so I figure he hasn't noticed. I wonder, if I had a side-boyfy sitting on my lap, would he notice?

Jix, standing on the other side of the Citroën, shielding his eyes against the sun, says, "You guys see what I see?"

We follow his gaze. At the end of the driveway, where it meets the road, a white man is sitting on a huge backpack. And I mean huge like belly-of-a-pregnant-hippo huge.

I ask, "Is this like the first hitchhiking Rhodie ever? In all Zimbabwean history?"

Swagga is cement-mixing with Fanta Orange, speaking around his mouthful of biltong and sweet drink. "He doesn't look down and out."

"He must be out of something."

"So . . . what," says Jix, "shall we give him a lift?"

"Why?" I ask.

"For all the great things that his ancestors brought to us."

"Very funny."

"Come on."

"Not in your shock absorber-free vehicle. We wouldn't want to hurt his tender backside."

"Look what my shawty only has on her mind . . . "

My slap hits his belly.

"Ouch."

We settle in and Jix starts the car. I feel a dread coming on at the thought of the ride ahead.

Jix is still musing. "He's not a Rhodie. I bet he's American or European."

"Maybe French," I volunteer.

"One more reason."

"Yeah, if he's a Frenchy, he deserves a ride in this car on these roads!" adds Swagga.

Jix backs out of the parking space. "Let's ask him where he's going," he says.

"And what? We don't know who he is. What if he turns on us after we give him a ride?" Me, I'm not a big fan of just picking up random people.

"I thought we were on an adventure," Jix says. "What could he possibly do to us? There's three of us, we can over-power him if he tries anything."

"And if he has a gun?"

"O-M-freaking-G, Chanda, where in your head do you live, honestly?" Swagga turns around to laugh in my face. "You can be so dramatic sometimes. You want to try some-thing different, then let's do something different, when else are we ever going to say we picked up a hitchhiker?"

"People hitchhike all the time in Harare, and I never see you stopping."

"Tjo! People in Harare are hectic, man, they'll 'jack you one time, bruh. Jix, swing left and let's give this man a ride."

"You're not the boss of this trip. I don't want some serial killer sitting in the back with me."

I'm really annoyed now, but Jix is already stopping and I clout Swagga in the back of his head with my palm.

"Eish! Violence, Chanda, violence."

I pull together all my stuff on the back seat to make a good-sized barrier between me and the guy who, against my strongly expressed wish, will come and sit with me. The least Swagga could do is change seats with me, but it doesn't look like an option he's considering. So far, sitting in the back, I was able to ignore the conversation up front if I wanted to, but now I will have to be friendly or sit in an uncomfortable silence with this Highway Killer. I kick the back of Swagga's seat for good measure. He just grins.

We pull up slowly beside the blond guy, causing as little dust around him as possible. He smiles at us, all psycho-friendly, while plotting how he will force us to stop in a remote spot and pull a chainsaw out of his hulking huge backpack and chop us all to pieces. Okay, so my imagination may be running a bit wild right now. Meanwhile Highway Chainsaw Killer is answering Swagga's question with a strong German accent. As a matter of fact, he sounds like Arnold Schwarzenegger with a good bite of schnitzel in his cheeks.

"I want to travel south, to South Africa," he says.

"Oan, you know you are in Zimbabwe right?" Swagga tells him.

"Yes, I touched down yesterday at Harare airport, a trucker gave me a lift here, a big misunderstanding."

"A freaking big misunderstanding, dude! Why didn't you fly straight to Jo'burg?"

"What?"

"Why didn't you fly straight to Johannesburg or Cape Town if you want to go to South Africa?"

"I want to travel the country."

We look at each other in disbelief.

Swagga says, "We're not going south."

"Doesn't matter."

"Where do you want to go then?"

"Doesn't matter, wherever."

Is this man crazy or what? He doesn't care where he is going, and if he doesn't have a place as a goal, maybe all he wants is to create an opportunity for his misdeeds. I mean, his story isn't even making sense—caught a flight to Harare because he wanted to go to South Africa! Travel the country by foot! Now doesn't care where he ends up? I whisper to Jix, "Hit the gas, let's go!"

But Jix says, "You know, we are going close to The Great Zimbabwe, it's a historic site, you may enjoy it."

I can't believe what I'm hearing. Enjoy it? Enjoy what? Slaughtering us?

"Sounds good," he answers.

I hiss, "Sounds like we'll all end up in a shallow grave."

Swagga gives me a look over his shoulder.

"Chillax girl," he hisses back.

"At least they can DNA us nowadays."

"Dude!"

"Throw your backpack in the trunk," says Jix to the man.

"Thank you!"

◆ ◆ ◆

The German pulls his door closed, sitting down beside me,

tall and muscular. He doesn't need a chainsaw for us, he can just choke the juice out of everybody.

"My name is Sven."

We introduce ourselves. Jix steers the car back onto the road.

"Hey, I have an idea," I tell Sven. "Would you mind? I'd like to film you introducing yourself. Is that okay?"

"You want to film me?"

"Yes, it's fun." And they will find the camera next to my rotten corpse in the bush and bust you for life, weirdo.

Swagga explains, "It's her hobby."

"More than my hobby."

"Okay."

I press the record button, and Sven gives a shrug, then freezes in front of the camera, a natural reaction for amateurs, even amateur psychopaths.

I ask him, "Well, who are you? What are you doing in Zim? What do you do in Germany? And what is in your backpack?"

He takes a deep breath, then says, "My name is Sven, Sven Draeger. I am on holiday, first time backpacking. In Germany, I finished school. I will start a . . . trainee program to be a mechanic in September and—what was the other question?"

"Your backpack! What is in your backpack?"

"A chainsaw."

The boys break into laughter. I almost lose my camera as the car swerves, that's how hard Jix is laughing.

Did he really say that?

"Oan, fist, bruh!" Swagga holds up his fist.

The German hits it with his wrecking ball of a hand—the universal language of irritating boys. I kiss my teeth loudly, 'cause I'm that pissed. They don't even notice.

"Oh, don't look like that, I'm joking," Sven says when they all stop their stupid laughing. "I packed way too much stuff."

Like I care!

"Now it's my turn!" demands Swagga-superstar and turns to me. I give him a nod and Sven turns a questioning look at Swagga.

"Uh hi, my name is Zwagendaba Moyo, known by all my associates as Swagga, 'cause you know I got it like that. Zwagendaba is the name of a Nguni king. So I think it's all just fitting. As you can see, I am completely swagalicious—okay, right now, I'm not in my dope ride and I don't have my rig on, the way I normally do, but we're kind of roughing it today. Uh, we're heading out to Gumindoga—wherever the hell that is, I hope we find it. Right now, we've just stopped to buy some refreshments at this ummm, let me say, establishment. We're just out of Chivhu now, been driving about three hours before that, and as you can see, it's gonna be a nice sunny day. Uh . . . okay, that's a wrap."

"I'm the director, Swagga, I say it's a wrap, not you."

"Eish bruh. Give me a break."

"Alrighty." I pan to Jix and I expect him to follow suit.

But he is covering his face with one hand. "Sorry, no filming permission," he says.

"Wha . . . ?"

"Nix, never, so turn it off."

"What's up?"

41

"I'm running a social experiment. If I don't exist digitally, do I really exist? Think about it. Except for birth certificate, ID, and passport, I'm currently just a statistic. How will nature preserve the real me? When anthropologists dig me up in the future, I want to be an enigma. Do you know, I've never been to the dentist, never broken a bone, and apart from when I was a kid, there are no photographs of me. The government only has my name and details of origin. As to who I am besides a statistic . . . Do you guys even know my government name? You call me Jix, and at home I am AJ to my folks. I don't even remember the last time anyone said my full name."

Dude is tripping.

"Hmh, and what about your cellphone, Facebook . . . Whatsapp . . . they all want your identity."

"They want *an* identity! And that's what they get. I have a dozen aliases. I'm the boy who is and always will be a ghost. I'm the Talented Mr Ripley as far as this life goes. Let's face it, you've known me for several years now, what do you actually know about me?"

To be honest, I can't say anything about him, apart from the fact that he lives in Mount Pleasant, he is eighteen, like Swagga, and drives a yellow Citroën. He has no favourite drink that I can recall, he doesn't smoke, he has no girl-friend—all negatives that say nothing else about him, just more of who he is not.

Now Sven the German must be thinking he is the one who could end up in the ditch. Haha!

I'm flabbergasted when he leans over the physical barrier between us and nudges my arm. "Now you."

42

"Huh?"

"Now it is your turn. It was your idea. Who are you?"

Dude is so forward, but there is no way you refuse to answer an interrogation delivered with a German accent. "Chanda," I tell him.

"Chanda, can I have the camera, so I can film you?"

I watch myself handing it to him. He turns it on and points it at me. I turn my face so the light comes from the side in a nice angle that will flatter my features and the no-longer fly hair, and start to speak.

"Hi, I'm Chanda. I am the social worker who accompanies these two delinquents on their excursions into society—"

A paper ball hits me from the front. We all laugh.

"Okay, no, seriously now, I am Chanda, and I'm going to visit the village my father comes from." I skip the memory and the zebra part and continue, "And I will stay there for a while, those two will head home probably tomorrow . . . "

"One hundred percent probably!" comes an answer from the front.

"And I don't know what I will do after this summer." And maybe I won't remember what I did this or any other summer before, and maybe this is good, that he is recording me introducing myself, since maybe I will forget who I am.

"That's a wrap. Cut."

THE GREAT ZIMBABWE—AND
LOST IN THE NOWHERE

The beats of Roki singing "Susanna" bounces in our eardrums. Jix had put on his favourite urban grooves CD when we left the last house in Chivhu behind us, an acoustic goodbye to civilization. Sven nods along to agree that indeed Susanna shouldn't be lying about the paternity of her child.

"So where are you going?" I ask him.

"Just travelling."

"Where would you like us to take you?"

"Wherever you're going is fine."

"What in particular are you trying to see while you are here?"

"Everything, anything."

"Dude, how can you just be like, whatever?"

"I'm living it one moment at a time, you never know what will happen next."

"May I film you for my show?"

"Sure."

"Do you like this music?"

"Sure."

OMG! This guy is on a level. He doesn't mind being filmed

and he likes Zim beats. He doesn't mind this, he doesn't mind that. He doesn't mind much of anything. But he's kind of cute, if you like blue-eyed, blond-haired butch. Not such a bad guy after all, and he's adding flavour to my little circus.

For a song length, everybody is quiet. Then Sven peeks over Jix's shoulder and says, "Is that 726,000 km?"

"Yep."

"Amazing, a Peugeot 504, built in, let me guess, 1981?"

"Citroën!" I correct him.

"Peugeot!" comes the boys' chorus from all around me.

"Jix, I thought you have a Citroën."

"Yeah, but one night it cocooned and turned into a beautiful Peugeot. No, it was always a Peugeot, since birth."

Well, fly me to Oz and call me Toto! I always thought it was a Citroën. Why did I think that?

Jix looks to Sven. "And you were pretty good, oan, it's an '82."

"Super."

"You are into cars?"

"Yes. Can I ask something?"

"Sure."

"What's *oan*? Is that good or not so . . . "

"That's good, oan, dude, bruh, like that. You're all right. What's your rig?"

"Huh?"

"What do you drive?"

"A Golf."

Swagga laughs out loud. "A golf cart?"

Jix and I laugh too, picturing big Sven in a golf cart on the German autobahn.

"VW Golf," he says.

Jix snaps his fingers. "Wait, that is a Rabbit, right? In Germany, the car is called something else. It's a VW Rabbit."

"Yes. Speaking of nature, where do we turn off the highway?"

"Right," I say and fish out my phone from my pocket. "Trim the beats, I have to make a phone call, asking for directions."

Winky D's dancehall narration of an encounter in a Jaguar has just faded into the sound of the engine when I hear Tete Frasia's "Hello."

"Good morning, Tete, it's me," I begin, my hand playing with the stone around my neck that she gave me.

"Chanda. How are you, my dear?"

"I'm well, if you are well, Tete."

"I am well, my dear."

"Tete, I need your help. I don't remember the exact way to Gumindoga."

There is a pause on the other end of the line and I hold my breath.

"What exactly do you remember?" she asks.

"Not much, to be honest."

"Ah. You are now on the highway?"

"Yes." I turn the speaker on so everybody can hear her and I won't be blamed if we get lost.

She says, "Follow the signs to Great Zimbabwe and take a left turn seven kilometres past the entrance. Stay on that road for a while, and when you get to two muzhanje after a big rock that stretches into a small river, you take a right there and head towards the setting sun."

We look at each other.

"Can you be a little bit more precise, Tete?"

"How can I possibly be more precise?"

"Like with road names and numbers."

She laughs. "Chanda, where do you think you're going—New York? Just listen to what I'm telling you and you'll be fine."

Listening to directions, right! Who does that anymore?

I just tell her, "Okay."

"Are you driving?"

"No."

"It's me," Swagga says.

"And me," Jix adds.

"And me." Sven being shy again. Not!

I could kill them, I actually should. All boys as a matter of fact.

Tete's voice is high with concern. "What are you doing? Are you in a Combi?"

"No Tete, don't worry. It's my friends . . . and a German."

"A German?"

"Ja!" Swagga says.

"What are you doing with a German?"

"Showing him our Great Zimbabwe." What else can I say?

I sense Tete filtering what's on her mind. "That's nice," she says finally, without conviction.

"Yes." What else?

"Do your parents know?"

"Uh, they know I'm on a trip."

Silence.

Sven's forehead crinkles a bit at my evasive tone. Ha!

Serves him right, getting into people's cars. I bet he's hoping this is not some shady runaway situation involving a minor that will bring him some time in a Zim jail cell.

"I left a letter explaining everything," I say.

"Dear, if they ask me I will tell them."

"Of course."

"And, boys?"

"Yes!" The boys chorus.

"Take good care of my girl!"

"Yes, yes, of course."

"Have a good time at Great Zimbabwe and in Gumindoga."

We thank her and say goodbye. I pack the phone away.

"Is this legal?" Sven says, his hand drawing an imaginary circle around us.

"What?" I ask. "Running away from home, robbing a bank, and taking a German hitchhiker as a hostage for ransom?"

We are laughing and joking around. We almost miss the sign for the Great Zimbabwe turn-off. I yell and Jix reacts like a race car driver, and the wheels spit gravel into the bushes. We all cheer.

The sun is still high and it's baking inside the car. Luckily for now, we have the windows open because there is a semblance of a tarred road ahead of us still. When we hit the dirt road, there will be fire and heat. At some point, according to Tete, we have to head towards the sunset. She could have said we should head west, which is just as bad, because who even has a compass? I'm not looking forward to that section of our journey. The sun is just about going to kill us, never mind the dust, which out here is something else.

"Next stop: The Great Zimbabwe."

❖ ❖ ❖

"Dude, imagine, this place has been here for hundreds of years and it's a standing testament to the greatness of our ancestors."

This is the most animated I have seen Jix. Usually it's like life is just so boring and predictable. But here I can actually feel some sort of excitement in him. "Imagine, dude, they left behind this amazing evidence of them having been here and what will we leave of ours? Discarded cellphone batteries and plastic to choke and poison those who will come after us. Can you imagine? How simple and how powerful their lives were back then—as close to nature as possible. Dude! They built all this without cement! See how thick these walls are." Jix hits at a wall with his palm and a small cloud of dust rises. The sound of his hand striking the stone wall is muted, in the narrow passageway that spirals in and up, around a conical tower. "No cement, bruh, just granite boulders and blocks. All we can do is find ways to stick things together somehow and still it all falls apart. So much for advancement."

Tjo! This is unprecedented. Would the real Jix please stand up? I wish I had caught him on camera. I pull it out.

The climb to the top of The Great Enclosure is a killer, the stone steps are uneven and sometimes not really steps at all, and the afternoon sun beats down on our heads with vengeance. I didn't think to bring a hat, I'm going to catch such a serious tan it's not even funny, but I don't want to be left behind by the boys. So we wind up the conical tower in single file, on the uneven stone steps. We don't really know anything other than what we read on a panel at the entrance, but it's liberating to be winding up to the top, stopping to run my hands over the stones, and catching my breath because sometimes I feel as if for real my lungs are going to just say, Stuff this, and collapse. But I make it, and we stand at the top, looking down at the networks of piled-up stone remains of ancient structures among flat patches of green grass and pale brown earth, no one structure complete anymore. I try to imagine the city that must have existed here, alive and bustling—outbuildings and huts scattered across the valley and the hillside, serving the great fort. In the distance is the misty horizon of Lake Kyle—a hazy blue stretch, and somewhere out there, too, is Gumindoga, where we should really try to get to before nightfall.

It's the right place for a quick video clip. I do a 360-degree pan: sparse vegetation, shrubs, and small thorn trees amidst the ruins, fading into the strangely misty lake horizon. The vidcam viewer finds Sven examining the stonework with his hands. "That's right," I say, "no cement, just stone on stone." Beside him, Jix is still excited, and I too feel like I'm in the right place somehow. I am not scared of the zebra, I haven't even thought about it all morning. For the first time in a long time, I am feeling like myself again. Hard to explain. Swagga strolls around with his hands in his pockets as if he arrived too late at the mall and all the shops are closed. I press STOP on the vidcam.

◆◆◆

Alas, the feeling from the great ruins doesn't last. After a reaffirming hour wandering around the ruins and exploring the small museum there, we hang out under a tree in the parking area and rehydrate. I'm beat. The walkabout and climb up to the tower has really kicked all our asses, and there isn't so much joking and talking anymore. When Jix gets behind the wheel again, we relax and let him drive, because we all heard and sort of understood Tete Frasia's directions, right? Wrong! The sun is beginning to set, and we have arrived at the gates of Zinetsa Secondary School for the third time since we left The Great Zimbabwe behind us. We took the turn seven kilometres after the entrance to The Great Zimbabwe, as Tete directed, but she said nothing about the school, and yet somehow here we are in front of it. Jix can't say how we got here, and naturally neither can Swagga. We have been driving in circles and everyone is now exasperated.

At the first go around, before we even knew we were lost, we encountered a small cluster of buildings that turned out be shops—Togara shops. Again, not one of Tete Frasia's landmarks, so how did we end up here? A total mystery. We thought maybe she hadn't given us all the landmarks, but we suspect that somehow we'd overshot the muzhanje trees where the big rock and the river are supposed to lead us to the right turn. At the shops, when we asked them where we were exactly, they said, "You are here at Togara shops and where is it you want to go?" I just died. The boys thought it was hilarious. Anyway, they gave us directions to the spot where Tete Frasia said there would be a small river and a bridge we should cross. We have seen no rock, no river, no bridge, but everyone we ask along the way assures us that we are heading in the right direction. What in the Twilight Zone is actually happening right now? For a minute everyone is quiet, then Jix steps out of the car. "Someone better make a plan soon, 'cause I can't keep driving in circles. We're wasting fuel."

"Jix, I told you to try that little road we passed back there. I'm sure it will take us in the right direction and we will see the river."

"That's not what that old guy said back there, he said keep going straight in this direction until you see a big msasa tree."

Swagga is leaning against the open passenger door, drinking the last of a lukewarm Red Bull.

Finally, Sven says something, contributing more than "sure" and "I don't mind." He says, "Ja, but the lady we spoke to before the shop said to take the left direction at the fork in the road. We did not see a fork in the road."

There is nothing worse than asking local people for directions. I don't know what goes through people's heads; even in Harare, nobody ever seems to know the names of streets, even though they always walk on them, so what hope do we have out here? I could just cry.

I lean out to speak to Jix. "Dude, I'm telling you. That's the only turn we haven't tried. Let's try it." I'm starting to panic a little. "Jix, just get back into the freaking car and take the direction I'm giving you."

Swagga gives me that look.

"Chill, bruh."

Absurdly, at that moment I have the thought that it's not so romantic that he calls me "bruh" all the time. I'm his girlfriend, damn it, and sometimes it would be nice to be treated that way. He turns to Jix, and I don't hear what he says to him, but Jix then literally throws himself back into the driver's seat and takes off like he's at a Grand Prix.

If I wasn't so pissed off, I would die laughing at Sven, who almost left his legs behind.

◆ ◆ ◆

Cue back to the scene in front of the school gates and multiply it by ten. As they say on TV, "Shit just got real."

After the undercarriage of the car scrapes over a stone for the hundredth time on possibly the worst excuse for a road, Jix hits the brakes, opens his door, and stalks off into the long grass before the damn thing has even fully stopped.

For a moment Swagga, Sven, and I remain quiet.

What the heck! It's the middle of freaking nowhere, the grass is so tall, it's like it's growing right back behind us as we move. Nobody would find us, even from a helicopter. It's so so quiet, except for the krrr-krrr sounds from the insects in the grass. We've been driving for a span without seeing anything, no river, nothing, it's just this little road going nowhere but deeper into the bush.

"Hey don't look at me. I don't know."

Of course, Sven is living in the moment and will go with whatever happens next.

Me, I'm tired and at this point I have nothing more to contribute. So I just sit back inside the car, close my eyes, and listen to Swagga muttering to himself outside. He is trying to find the one bar of signal he'd caught earlier, so he can use his phone, although I don't know who he's planning to call.

It's become so stressful, I am feeling like maybe if I close my eyes and do a little meditation I will feel how I felt earlier. It's going on to five o'clock.

◆ ◆ ◆

I wake up, my heart thumping in my chest. I am running. The high grass is whipping at my face. Everything is wrong and I have to get away. Somewhere in the background I can hear someone calling me, but it's like I'm in a tunnel and it's collapsing on me from behind. I have to get to the light I can see at the end, before I suffocate. And so I am running and running, and the grass is whipping at me, and thorny bushes are tugging at my clothes and scratching my skin, but I don't care and when I finally stop it's like my eyes are open for the first time.

Everything around me is new, the grass is shorter, the ground is rockier and transitions into a steep slope. Good that I stopped, I would have gone tumbling down to God knows where. I have no idea where I am or what I am doing. I can't remember how I got here. I must be dreaming. But the burn in my chest is very real and I can hear my breathing in a way that I never do in dreams. No, I am here.

The trick is not to panic. Take deep breaths and focus. I should retrace my steps. There's a clear gap in the grass where I came thundering through. I walk back there, but what was I running from, and OMG, where the hell am I? I tell myself not to panic as I feel the tears in my eyes. There has to be a reasonable explanation. And then I see it, a flash of white from the corner of my eye, black stripes and long-lashed eyes in a horsey face between the leaves. The zebra disappears as I try to approach it, only to appear a little further away, stepping out of a thicket and looking back at me. I keep going towards it, back the way I came. I know I must follow the zebra.

Again I find that I have left the tall grass behind, and before I know it, I am looking down into a valley stretching all the way to the horizon: brown and flat, rocky mountains behind it in the far distance. From where I am in the dusky light, I can just make out dotlike dwellings around a wide space in the middle of which stands a large tree with a big branch running almost parallel to the ground. Just how Tete Frasia described it. It all comes rushing back.

❖ ❖ ❖

"Dude!" That's all Swagga says and shakes his head when I return to the car. You'd think he'd hug me or something. Classic Swagga—when things get tense, he pulls back like a tortoise until the danger's passed. It's not that he doesn't care, he's just . . . Swagga.

Jix is in the driver's seat, arms around the steering wheel, head down, as though taking a nap. He looks up as I open the door and slide in. Sven looks at me as if nothing at all happened.

"You scared us," Swagga says.

"I have seen the village and I have an idea how to get there," I pronounce.

They exchange looks without saying a word. I don't know how, but I feel that I know the direction we should take. They see that.

"Let's keep going and somewhere just ahead, the grass will chill with the growing, the scenery changes, and we will have a better view of where to go from there."

I can't explain it and I'm not even going to try. It seems just more of what has been happening to me lately. I have always been someone who plans things to the last eventuality, I make sure things work the way I want them to. But in the last couple of months, this has all just fallen apart and I've not been able to be in control. Well, now I think I'm going to take control, and who knows, we may just get to where we are going.

❖ ❖ ❖

As Jix bumps along, swearing under his breath at the abuse of his car, I sit back and think about what happened a few minutes ago. Did I fall asleep for like a minute and start dreaming? Either that or my brain was gathering data on automatic and came to some frightening conclusion. Rumbi always tells people that I am one of those who has a long fuse, and when it blows, it's always unexpected. Even I never know when it's all going to go to hell. It's been happening a lot in the last few weeks, but I know one thing for sure, I'm not crazy and I don't want Rumbi and John to pay someone who can't tell me more.

When we finally make it through the sea of grass, it's like finding civilization again; we pass little homesteads, a store here and a store there, donkeys, carts—who knew people still lived like this?—and then we see the river.

Jix is back in a good mood and already pontificating about going back to the simple life. Life itself! Harare is just a big city. Big cities are like smartphones, lots of apps but little life! We in the city are really going to suffer when the machine stops.

"I don't think it will happen in our lifetimes, Jix," I tell him.

"Of course it won't, we are ensuring the slow and unavoidable death of the human species while changing its nature, so that by the time the last humans die out, we will resemble nothing like how we began. I want to be organic, dust to dust, remembered only by nature and not by machines. I don't want to be part of some e-history and have my life story represented by Facebook and government recordings of my conversations. Have any of you ever been to the post office to mail a letter?"

"What for, when there's email, Snapchat, Twitter, FaceTime, WhatsApp . . . need I go on?" Swagga asks.

Jix shakes his head. "A letter is a real thing. You can hold it. A person sat down and thought about what they wanted to say and took time over it. Maybe with doodles on the side. It's not some consonants and numbers welded together while someone is driving or walking. It's not a Like button."

"This is true," says Sven, not to be left out. "Me too, I'd enjoy letters and receiving things in the post. It is special. I want to send postcards to my family and friends."

I think Jix has found a new BFF. Shame on poor Swagga, he's stuck with me as both his BFF and GF now. Or the other way round.

The so-called bridge is a cement pathway across a stream, wide enough for one car to cross at a time. Of course, none of us knows the dangers and challenges of a rural bridge, especially when there is water flowing over it.

Jix, still waxing lyrical about organic existence, charges his Peugeot straight at the bridge, and all four of us fly off our seats as it hits something hard—a pothole—and smash our skulls against the roof. If that weren't enough, water rises above the tires, and of course the current is stronger than we thought. For the first time Sven shows some emotion and says, "Oh this is not good!" And I rub the top of my head, with the thought that this would never have happened had we brought Swagga's car. This journey has become a disaster, and we are getting washed away.

Somehow the car keeps moving forward and Jix slams his hands on the steering wheel, yelling, "Yes, yes, yes!"

The Peugeot makes it out of the water and rolls down the road a couple of kilometres or so, before shuddering to a stop.

Jix swears and gets out, Sven follows him to the hood. They bend over it, fiddle around with the engine, look underneath the car, while conferring with each other like two surgeons about to perform surgery on the devil's mother at gunpoint.

It's nice where we are, but the light is almost gone. The dirt road here is fairly wide, and we can see clearly where it leads. We must be close to the homestead, because we have been driving awhile towards the village. I walk a little way through a copse of msasa trees and thorn bushes that seems to stretch on for quite a bit, and I'm sure that just beyond them must lie the Tiregeyi homestead.

In a small clearing, not far from the road, I'm putting my vidcam away in its pouch and securing the straps over my shoulders when I hear it. A kind of barking. For a minute I think, ah shit, dogs, wild dogs, I'm so outta here, but for some reason I hesitate, thinking that it doesn't quite sound like any dog in my experience. Suddenly the grass to my left parts and I see the biggest baboon. He sits there on the ground looking at me as if making up his mind about something. I don't need to think, my legs carry me and that's that. I run, faster than I have ever done in my life, not taking a single breath in or out until I've landed on the back seat of the Peugeot. By the time the guys turn to see what I'm running from, there's a troop of baboons loping down the road in our direction.

I am just about killed from the way Swagga jumps up from where he's lounging against the car. In between trying to catch my breath and dying of laughter I almost pass out. By the time I can breathe normally again, we are all in the car, doors locked and windows rolled up.

"Shit! Chanda you're not right. You don't even warn others," Swagga says.

"Eish, sorry bruh. I didn't think."

"Tjo! Look at these oans bruh. They look like they can just klap you one time and you'll be bust."

Jix's eyes are huge in his thin face and he is breathing hard.

Sven is laughing, red in the face. "Just monkeys!" he says.

"Just monkeys?" Jix exclaims. "I have come across the same before and let me tell you, they are terrorists. Last year I was over in Kariba with my peeps and they came into the place we were staying. When I walked into the kitchen, Mr Baboon had opened the fridge. When he heard me, he turned around and the expression on his face! The grin of death. I tell you, I just said, 'Sorry, dude, carry on,' and I closed the door and waited for him to leave. The owner told us later that they once had to renovate the entire cottage after they forgot to close a window after a long weekend, and a bunch of baboons went all cray cray in there."

"Come on, monkeys. I know them from the zoo," Sven insists.

"Dude, this ain't a German zoo!" Swagga replies.

"What's the big difference?"

"What's the . . . What's the . . . did he just . . . ? I tell you what's the big difference. The big difference from your zoo puppies is, these fellas ain't fed and have no medical plan."

We have a situation here. Three big baboons and a few little ones have come closer and are messing about around the car. The three big ones are on all fours, fists planted as if to say, check out how hard we are, we walk on our knuckles.

I've heard that after they slap you with those hands of theirs, you think you're one of them.

They're staring at us over the hood that Jix and Sven didn't shut, simply propping up the cover with a wrench. Now it seems one of the smaller baboons has found a better use for the wrench, because it's galloped off into the grass with it. The hood miraculously stays up, so maybe the wrench was actually serving no good purpose at all, and the baboon deserves its new toy.

I'm just hoping it doesn't come back and bang on our

windows with that thing. The windows are our only protection right now. The big ones—especially the King Kong alpha male—are staring us down, and we are staring helplessly back like some lip-syncing band at a press conference while a journalist blows their cover. By this time I remember to turn on my vidcam, but it's going to be crap footage because my hand is shaking and the light is low.

"Does anyone have a gat?" Swagga whispers.

"You want to shoot them?" Sometimes Swagga's ideas are plain crazy. Which one of us would just be hanging out with a gun?

"That's not an answer to the question I just asked."

"Oh sure, I keep one on me for occasions like this, the new pocket baboon-bazooka! Come on."

Sven clears his throat and for one horrified moment I think he is about to produce a gun. But he just says, "I think we're . . . am Arsch."

"Umm Orrsh?" echoes Swagga.

"Uh . . . "

"You mean the f-word?"

"Yes, the f-word, but all caps!"

"Oh! I thought you said they were just monkeys," I say sweetly.

Sven takes a good look at King Kong and says, "Well maybe I take your version of things this time. You know your Zimbabwean monkeys best." He gives me a slightly mocking smile. I ignore him.

"We need to scare them away," Swagga says.

That's when it happens. Maybe Sven has just had a vivid flashback of his German ancestors fighting back the Roman legions, 'cause he pushes open his door, jumps out of the car, spreads out his arms, and performs a Bavarian version of the New Zealand haka dance, producing sounds with his mouth that he might've heard in the darkest corner of his German zoo.

When King Kong propels himself in his direction, it takes Herman the German Maori only a fraction of a second to be back on his seat in the car, slamming the door shut.

Jix stammers, "Dude . . . dude, what was that?"

"I thought . . . phew . . . it would scare them away."

"King Kong thought you were ready for mating."

Jix and I laugh with nervous relief. It's funny but also not funny.

"Hmh."

"Where did you learn that . . . tactic?"

"For the record, you Germans are known for many things, and correct me if I am wrong, improvisational skills aren't one of them."

"I guess."

Swagga mutters something about European tourists' stunts that get them chowed by lions.

Just then, a stroke of genius. Jix presses his fist on the hooter, and at the first loud honk, the baboons scatter, even the hard oans who had been terrorizing us just with their stance. Although I have to say that for a moment they looked as if they weren't convinced they were in any danger, probably because of Sven's performance. They hover at the sides of the road for a minute, but then they decide in favour of caution, and turning their pink asses up at us they saunter back into the longer grass and disappear.

"Why didn't you do that when I was out there?" Sven asks.

"Because maybe you would have just run with your friends into the bush!"

When we calm down from all the laughter, I ask, "What do we do now? The car is bust. It's dangerous out there and it's getting dark."

"I think we should try and walk the rest of the way. You say we are close, no?"

Sven must be in a state of shock, suggesting that. This is exactly why things happen to foreigners over here, they are too brave. Walk? Is he for real?

"Ahhh jack bruh! Are you out of your mind?"

I know Swagga won't go for that. But Jix, Sven's NBFF displays his new allegiance.

"We don't have a choice. Well, the only other choice is to sleep here tonight."

I'm down with that. I'm thinking that maybe the baboon militia is lurking out there somewhere, just waiting for us to come out, grinding their fists into their palms in anticipation of a smackdown. No thanks.

We're all about ready to just take the chance when we see the silhouette of someone walking up the road, big stick in one hand and a hulking dog at his side. Things are either about to get worse or, hoping against hope, better.

THE VILLAGE—AND WHERE IS MY PHONE?

I t's a local oan, young, about our age, and in the fading light he looks threatening. He's wearing a T-shirt that says "Get a Life!" and for a minute I can't help thinking it's directed at me. He peers into Swagga's window and smiles at us. He knocks on the window, and Swagga rolls it down.

"Greetings," he says in formal Shona and Swagga responds in kind. It's funny to hear him switch from his slang tones to his decent-person voice. I am forced to do the same when the boy greets me. And when his turn comes, Sven repeats our Shona replies in an accent impossible to describe, but he is understandable, so I guess it's okay.

"I heard you hooting from down the road. Are you in some kind of difficulty?"

I speak up quickly just in case Jix or Swagga decide to be macho and dismiss the help we desperately need. "Yes. Our car has broken down and we are looking for the home of the Tiregeyi."

"You are not too far. I was heading back there from the fields when Fiso and I had to chase a band of baboons that were tampering with my crops."

I think he knows exactly what happened before he

arrived on the scene, but is too polite to let us know. For a moment, none of us speaks a word and we stare at our visitor. We can hardly believe that we have finally found the place.

"If you are coming, we had better get going. It is not too far, but it's still a bit of a walk and these days it's not safe to be roaming around at night—we are having a small problem with wildlife."

The fact that he's walking around so confidently with those baboons hanging around close by makes my mind up for me, and Fiso looks reassuringly assertive. The dog looks to me like a Rhodesian Ridgeback, and I have to say I have always liked that type of dog, they're very handsome. I feel safer with this one guy than with the three I came with. I scramble to get my stuff.

"Just bring what you can carry easily. We can come back for the rest tomorrow. Don't worry, no one will touch your car. Just make sure you lock the doors—Sekuru and his gang might come back, and those guys are too clever for their own good."

Sekuru—Uncle—I immediately realize is the big baboon who was in the middle of the pack, staring down at us. King Kong. In the stories about the hare and the baboon that Tete Frasia would tell me when I was little, she always called the baboon Sekuru Gudo.

The guys also start putting their stuff together. Swagga wants to bring the cooler box, but none of the rest of us is willing to hold the other handle, so he is forced to leave it. Sven throws stuff out of his backpack into the trunk and shoulders his half-empty beast.

Once we are all out of the car and ready to go, the guy turns to us and, placing his arm across his chest in the respectful gesture that I sometimes see Shona men doing when greeting each other, he introduces himself: "My name is Vimbiko."

He is obviously what we call back in town an SRB—Strong Rural Background. He doesn't use the Shona slang we use back in Harare to make speaking to each other more hip and fun. I don't think any of us really speak formal and proper Shona.

After the introductions, long exchanges that end with the words "I am happy to make your acquaintance," we set off down the road. No one wants to be the last in line so we all sort of huddle together in a group and try to keep as close to Vimbiko and Fiso as possible.

❖❖❖

Rural rule number 1: Never trust a person who says, "It's not far." It takes us some thirty minutes to get to the homestead, and by the time we arrive it is properly dark, and I am wishing that I had worn my sneakers instead of my little ballet pumps. There's no such thing as rural chic, I tell you. It's best to be just practical. The elasticated pumps have rubbed my feet raw, at the back and in front over the bunion joint. Next to me Swagga is now just shuffling along, having tired of hoisting up his pants. Only Jix and Sven appear unbothered.

Vimbiko calls out as we approach the first dark shape, which I take to be the kitchen, judging from the flicker of a fire inside and the smoke escaping the open door. I see little shadows running around outside a square brick building with a veranda. A couple of dogs bark. By their shadows they look like typical rural dogs—skinny, vicious mongrels. I hear men's voices and realize there are people sitting on the veranda on chairs. I'm struck by how strange it feels, to be here right now. Twenty-four hours ago, I was back home lying on my bed, watching Netflix on a plasma screen in the middle of Harare. We left home this morning and we are now in a place that is so far removed from our everyday life that we couldn't have imagined it, amidst people we don't know. Did I really do the right thing? Two friends and a foreigner risking their well-being for me.

Maybe I should have convinced Tete Frasia to come with me instead. For her it would have been a nice trip. These are her people, and even though they are also related to me, they are strangers. I don't even know what to say to them. Tete Frasia said to ask for her sister, Tete Victoria. I think she's her cousin-sister, not her same-mother-same-father sister. She said their fathers were brothers. Apparently this Tete Victoria has knowledge of healing and things of a more mystical—or demonic as John would say—nature. She will know what is happening to me and what the zebra means. I just want to get back to normal. I don't need to subscribe to these beliefs, but I want my old life back. I have big plans and they don't include black spots or zebras and other apparitions.

Vimbiko cups his hands and claps them together before stooping to enter the kitchen. Right. We have to remember our manners, most of which we have abandoned—well I, at any rate, because Rumbi and John don't entertain our relatives very much and everyone we deal with is very lax about these traditions.

By an unspoken unanimous decision the four of us decide to wait outside. How do these people survive in this darkness? I would have thought that the rural electrification program had brought ZESA to everyone in the country by now. I have to say, though, that at this point I am sort of used to the dark and can actually see things here and there.

I bend down to look for my cellphone in my satchel when someone comes rushing out of the hut and without any warning I find myself wrapped in a smoky, sweaty embrace and being jogged up and down like a packet of popcorn.

"Heeeeee, wauya maDube! Our grandmother has come back to us! VaTiregeyi has returned!"

Okaaay! I don't know what to say, but I think I'm not required to speak yet. The lady is going on. I'm just amazed at how she managed to single me out in the dark.

"Is it really you, our grandmother's namesake? After all these years. Now a grown woman, come back to your father's home to see your people. Welcome. Welcome. Come in."

The invitation is issued at the same time as I get pulled into the hut. She pushes me down on a mat that feels smooth, and the guys are made to sit on a low ledge that runs along the wall, where Vimbiko is already seated, very much at home. Smoke stings my eyes and I breathe slowly so I don't start coughing.

"Amai!" My abductress, who I guess is my fifth or sixth cousin, is leaning towards an ancient woman seated on the floor in front of a kitchen unit mounted with cups and plates and various other things.

"Amai. It is Chandagwinyira, John's daughter. She's come to visit us. She's brought her friends."

It's not too obvious, but I see the resemblance to Tete Frasia in the old woman's face. She is much older though, her face is more weathered, and she appears to be somewhat stooped. She looks towards me, almost as if she can't really see, or as if she is sort of looking past me or into me, it's a bit weird. And putting her forefinger and thumb to her nose she takes a deep sniff of what I guess is snuff.

"Heya, it's Chandagwinyira. VaTiregeyi. Mawuya amaDube. Welcome back home. And where is the John of it? Your father? You have come here with just your friends?" asks Tete Victoria.

"Yes, Tete. My father is at home in Harare," I reply in my most respectful voice. It comes naturally, it's the only way to be. Something about the old lady has rendered me meek. The other lady is fine, she is full of energy and bubbly and happy, it's easy to be normal around her.

Tete Victoria's fingers reach out for me and she touches my necklace. "Nice, very nice." She looks in the direction of the boys. "And who are your people? What is your totem so we can greet you?"

Swagga goes first and I'm surprised at his good manners—I think he saves them for when he knows he won't get away with anything else—a kind of conservation of energy. Just as Vimbiko did as he entered the hut, Swagga cups his palms and claps them together lightly to show respect before speaking in front of the elders. Who knew? Eish! Me, I just spoke. I really should have known better.

"With your permission, my elder, I am Zwagendaba Moyo of the Dhehwa. Our home is kwaMurambi in Gokwe."

"Welcome Dhehwa Moyondizvo, the ones who milk cows, the ones who welcome subjects, you, Sahayi the lion, keeper and master of the earth. Welcome you people of Bhasvi, those who bring down the rain, King who does not stretch his legs, if he stretched them out the rain would turn to mist. Welcome."

Wow! These are Swagga's peeps. No wonder he's too cool for school—King who does not stretch his legs—yes, this is true.

Everyone in the room claps their cupped palms together, including me. This much is automatic. When the clapping starts on occasions such as this, just join in. Even Sven gets it and claps his hands.

"And you?" She looks at Jix.

"I am Soko, of Hwedza."

"Welcome Soko, white hair, the pompous one, those who come from Guruuswa, those who come from Hwedza, who obtained chieftanship through shrewdness and diplomacy, those always on the cliffs, who refused to till the land, the pompous one, welcome."

Ha! Jix the pompous one. Again we clap our cupped palms together, the sound is really great—a percussion of ancestral air. When the sound dies down, Tete Victoria continues, "You are our son-in-law then. There is another of your people in this village. He married Cremencia, old Nhamoinesu's daughter. The family had no sons and so he agreed to live here with his wife to help care for the old ones left. Welcome mukwasha. This too is your home."

Then her attention turns to Sven.

"And you?"

Sven imitates both Swagga and Jix with the hands and says, "I am Sven. I come from Germany."

Uproarious laughter erupts. Everyone is really tickled that Sven has spoken to them half in Shona, half in English peppered with his Germanesque tone.

"Ah, he speaks Shona!" Cousin is astounded. "Is he really from across the seas?"

"Yes," I say, "he is our friend who is travelling with us. He is learning about our country pretty fast, fast like a German car." It's best if we don't reveal that we met Sven only today.

"He is wise, to learn the language of a place in which he is a visitor," Tete Victoria says finally. She is smiling at him and continues to speak to him in Shona, oblivious that he may not understand.

"Welcome Sven, from far across the sea, men without knees, those who brought lightning sticks and sugar, those who sail far from their ancestors. Welcome."

Although she has gone beyond Sven's knowledge of the language, he smiles anyway and claps along. Nobody bothers to translate for him. He's going to have a fine time here with his German and English.

"How are things where you are coming from?" she asks me.

"All is well, Tete."

"Your parents?"

"They are well. They send greetings."

I can tell she doesn't believe me.

"And my sister, how is she?"

"Tete Frasia is fine, she sent me to you."

"Ehe-e."

When Cousin adds another log to the fire and the smoke billows out again, I am just done. My eyes start to water seriously and I can't stop the coughing. Cousin laughs and says, "Ah shame, shame, little mother, you are not used to the smoke. Go and get some fresh air outside. I'll bring the food to you when it is ready. Don't worry, after a while it won't affect you at all."

❖ ❖ ❖

Jix, Swagga, Sven, and Vimbiko follow me as I leave the hut and Vimbiko shows us a bench under a tree where we can sit. It's actually not so dark that we can't see the other people moving about. It's nice outside; there's a cool breeze and only a faint hint of woodsmoke, my eyes and lungs thank me. I look up and the sky is so potted with stars that I feel dizzy for a moment. Shamazing! I could just lie down somewhere and lose myself in the vision above me. I mean, we see stars in suburbia but this . . . this is everything. Jix, standing next to me, says, "Uh-huh! Now this is what I'm talking about, 'beam me up, Scotty.'" That might not be a bad idea—I chuckle quietly at the thought. Jix would fit right in up there, being all alternative, boldly going forth to new worlds and stuff.

Before we are quite settled, Cousin comes to say we should greet the other people in the village. Among them are an uncle—Tete Victoria's brother—and four more cousins, two male and two female, and there are the little kids who don't stay in one place long enough for you to remember them. They are possessed with built-in night vision, running around everywhere in the darkness. Everyone is at great pains to tell me who they are in the grand scheme of things, but I don't know any of the people they are using as their reference points. Eish! I don't know my own family. I am different things to all of them—to one I am aunt, to another I am daughter, to another I am niece, and to one I am even amai, mother. Okay, this I get, it's my culture, but for the life of me I can't keep it straight in my head. Who I am to someone explains which side of my family they come from and how we're related, but in order to remember, I need a chart of some sort, so I just nod and smile and say, "Yes, how are you. Yes. Yes. Ehe. Okay."

It's a strange thing, all my relatives always seem to know me, but I don't know them. By the time Cousin brings out the food, my stomach has tied itself into knots munching away at itself. It growls at the smell of peanut butter sauce. She's brought three plates, one with a heap of steaming sadza—grain-dumpling—another with something like peanut butter stew, and one with green vegetables. A little kid with a runny nose brings us a dish of water to wash our hands. Cousin tells me I will have to eat outside with the boys, until I can get used to the smoke and eat in the kitchen with her and the other women. Eee! I'm glad I get to stay out here with my friends, and I don't know any longer if it was such a hot idea to come running here where I don't really know people.

The boys dig in, and even though I am hungry, I approach the food with caution. I form my ball of sadza with my fingers and dip it into the sauce. I feel something with my fingertips, it's sort of spongy and I have a sinking feeling what it might be.

"Hey Swagga, what's the meat, bruh?"

"Hmm?" Swagga is happily munching away.

"What is in the sauce?"

"I don't know, but it's kicking." No help there. I'd forgotten that Swagga will eat just about anything.

"It's kind of chewy, almost like a Bavarian white sausage." Thanks, Sven.

"Dude, if you're hungry, eat. It's nourishment."

That's not going to happen with me. It's madora, I just know it and I bet Swagga knows it too, and he knows how much I hate worms. I can't even look at one, much less eat it.

"Swagga, you suck!"

I'll have to stick to the greens. They turn out to be pumpkin leaves fried with tomato and onion and a bit of chili. Delicious—these I can eat, but I know I will be hungry later.

"Don't worry, your highness," says Jix. "I bought some biltong at the service station where we stopped, I will share it with you when I get to my stuff." He's being snarky, but I'm relieved, and because of that I refrain from calling him Soko, the white-haired pompous one. I hope he bought a lot of biltong, because if mopane worm is what is likely to be the regular meat on the menu here, I will need a stock that goes a long way.

◆ ◆ ◆

Although they have solar lights here, you can't have them on all night, and there are only three of them. After Cousin takes me to the room where I will sleep, she takes her lamp with her. We have been put in the brick house. One of the uncles from the city built it for his family to stay over the holidays. Cousin, her kids, and Tete share a room, my three friends share a room with Vimbiko, and I have the pleasure of my own company. Anyone else would be happy. Not I. I hate the dark. I am also afraid of fire, but when I die, I would still rather be cremated than have to lie in a coffin in the dark. That's how much I hate the dark. I don't like to eat worms, nor should they eat me.

There's a sort of lounge outside my room, and there's even a bathroom with a tub and a shanks, but there's no running water. Vimbiko said everyone uses the bathing shacks outside, where there are some sort of solar showers. Some go to the river to bathe, and from what I can smell sometimes, one or two don't choose any of the options above. Just like in H.

The assorted cousins all have their own rooms in the other rondavels—round huts—clustered around the homestead.

Now everyone has gone to bed and it's quiet. It's so dark I can't even see my hand in front of my face. And let me just tell you about this bed. There is a hole in the mattress right about where my bum is. A hole. So, right now, I am lying on my back with my bum in some weird depression in the bed under the sheet and I am greatly disturbed.

Mattress and blankets smell musty.

Let Jix call me your highness, whatever, I don't like other people's things next to my skin or around me. I haven't taken off my jeans and hoody and I've kept my socks on, but still, this whole scene is just not working for me. In the middle of the night, my belly acts up. Intestinal wahala is not what I need here, where the only usable toilet is a field march away through the dark. I try to fall asleep again. My body doesn't think so. No way, my gut tells me. Nothing helps. I get up and search on the floor for my pumps, which I positioned so they would be ready at a moment's notice.

Cousin showed me where the toilet was, just in case . . . and in case has come to pass.

I sneak out and start picking my way through the long grass. Me going to blair toilet—at night, in the bush, by myself! My feet ache from a day in ballet pumps and my heart is pounding as I walk through long scratchy grass and bushes and around little trees, all the while imagining what could possibly fall into my hair from those branches, not to mention hairy caterpillars hanging around like they tend to do. The light of the moon isn't enough for my fearful fantasy, so I use the flashlight on my phone—which I wisely put in my pants pocket before going to bed—to light the way. Rushing shadows everywhere, anyway.

I smell the toilet long before I see it in the dark. From here I could find my way with closed eyes just following my nose. I gag. There are the two toilets next to each other, one for men and the other for women, surrounded by concrete walls. I step into one and almost fall right into the hole in the floor. Hell to the NO! Gagging galore. I have no choice, unless I want to take it outside. And I have to squat.

All I'm thinking is what I might be exposing my bare bum to, over the abyss. Moths flutter in the torchlight of my phone. An oily mud shimmers deep down in the hole. Why couldn't they have just put a toilet seat over it to make it easier for some of us? I don't know why I expected there to be any tissue, of course there is none. Drip-dry situations are not my thing. But what to do? I waddle out into the dark and by my phone light gather enough leaves that have no thorns or spikes, or spiders, caterpillars, or worms, and make my way back to the toilet. OMG, classic. I'm so glad I came by myself. I cannot imagine any way that I would ever live this down with the boys. The last leaf has just found its use when something falls into my hair.

I bet they can hear me screaming all the way back home at 21 Addison Close. Jumping up, I lose my grip on the phone and it is swallowed by the abyss underneath me. I scream a few decibels louder—I really don't know why at this point, I'm just so freaked out by everything and before I can think rationally I find that I have hit the road without pulling up my jeans or anything.

Panicking doesn't solve anything, but the rational part of me left the smelly dungeon long before me. Next thing I know I come to a stop behind our house and I'm pulling up my pants and collecting my dignity. My mouth produces sounds as if I am drowning in cold water while I'm scruffing my hair to shreds until I have inspected every single track of my weave. I must look as though I have survived a light-ning strike. I'm so revved up. How in the hell will I go to sleep after this?

At least nobody has seen me.

❖ ❖ ❖

I must have fallen asleep anyway because I find myself waking up to a sound. Still dark outside—just excellent.

I'm thinking, oh no, the zebra again, when I hear a whirring. I swear that if I have never been still in my life before, I am a stone right now. I think I have even stopped breathing.

Whrrrrrr, whrrrr, whrrrrr.

Sort of rhythmic. What the hell? This night is one big horror show.

Whrrrrrr, whrrrr, whrrrrr.

My eyes almost fall out of their sockets straining against the dark. I can't see anything.

Whrrrr, whrrrr, whrrrrr.

Like someone swinging one of those funny toys around their head on a string.

Whrrrr . . .

And that something stirs the air around my face. I am so outta here!

I don't even know how I find the floor, it's so dark I can hardly tell which way is up but right now if I need to, I will fly. I don't even make a sound, I just head for the door to the boys' room and dive in. Literally, because as I step over the threshold, I trip over something and land on a warm body on the floor.

The funny thing is, apart from an "oof" of air leaving my body as I land, there is very little sound; or maybe in my state I have been struck deaf, I don't know, all I know is that I have found someone. It's Vimbiko. I can tell right away, because the body I have draped myself around is built. It definitely is not Swagga, and somehow I know it's not Sven.

Nobody else stirs. I can hear snoring and deep breathing and the room smells of sleeping boys without sneakers.

"Chanda?"

"Yes it's me." My voice comes out in a small whisper.

"What's this?"

"There's something in my room."

He starts laughing and I feel a bit annoyed.

"It's not funny. It's dark, I'm scared. Stop laughing."

He frees himself from the blankets and in the process dislodges me.

"Let's go see."

"No. I'm not going anywhere inside there with the abominable whirr-animal."

"Come on."

He takes my hand and pulls me up. "I'll get a lamp."

It's on the table in the lounge. He lights it and walks into my room. I follow, hiding behind him.

"Aha!" he says, holding up the lamp. I see nothing but a dark spot in a corner.

"It's just chiremwaremwa."

I'm not sure what he is saying, I know this word, but I have to search in my vault for its meaning.

What! A bat? There's no such thing as *just* a bat. It's a freaking bat! In the same room as me. Flying around like it's nobody's business.

"It won't do anything to you."

"I don't care. I'm not sleeping in here."

"You will go to Tete and Amai Roddy?"

Amai Roddy? For a minute I'm lost, then I remember, that's what Cousin is called. She's Rodwell's mother, Rodwell who is one of the little kids we saw earlier.

No, I won't go in there. I feel uncomfortable at the

thought of having to wake them up and finding a place for myself somewhere in their sleeping arrangements. So I just kind of stand there and look at Vimbiko. I'm surprised that no one else has woken up. It's deathly quiet, I'm sure some-one will hear us, but it must be the fresh air or something 'cause people seem to sleep like the dead around here. I remember this from childhood, strangely enough. It would have been easier if Cousin had woken up then, I could make a plan with her. But I suspect even trying to wake her up will be a mission.

"I'll just come and sleep with you guys." Right there I wish I could have phrased that somewhat differently.

He smiles and wants to say the inevitable. Boys are all the same.

I stop him with, "Shut up."

The thought of sharing the small room with four fart-ing, snoring boys is not very attractive. Plus, I seem to have been given the guest room that has a bed, such as it is, but the boys are sleeping on reed mats on the floor.

"It won't do. You cannot share a room with boys. It will not be well received."

"Nobody needs to know."

"It's just not done."

The thing about Vimbiko is that he speaks purely in Shona and it's strange to me. I feel uncomfortable talk-ing to someone my age in such undiluted Shona, and I am answering him in a mixture of English and slangish Shona. It's okay when I am talking to older people because that's just the way it's always been. Anyway, to my suggestion, Swagga would have just said, "Don't get mad if you wake up and things are poking you," or something as lame. Vimbiko is of the old school.

"I will get rid of the bat for you and you can sleep with the lamp on. I will charge it in the morning."

He hulks about, swinging a grass broom in the air like a weapon, until the bat does a fly-by over my head and into the lounge, then out the front door, which Vimbiko has opened for this purpose.

"There," he says, smiling, "no more bat. Goodnight."

I grab the lamp and shut the door in his face. Again, I wish I hadn't come. I'm hungry, my bunions ache, and I feel dirty. Tomorrow, if the car can be fixed, I will go back to Harare with the boys. I cannot imagine spending another night in this bed, in this darkness and dirt. What was I thinking?

TETE VICTORIA

Morning comes without warning. For a moment I don't know where I am. Stiff, I stretch my arms and legs and my heart is beating like I'm on acid or something. The roof is spinning and nothing makes sense. What time is it? I can't find my phone. It's not beside the bed, not in my pockets, my shoes, between the sheets, or in the hole of the mattress.

"What the . . . "

My back aches. I can barely straighten myself. I feel grubby and wrinkled. I don't recommend sleeping in skinny jeans, I feel like stuffed sausage meat.

I look out the small window by the bed. Outside, the birds are loud and a dog is barking. It's light. I hear voices, children calling to each other, and someone is laughing. I see the homestead for the first time by daylight—no manicured lawns and beds of flowers like back home, just a wide space of cleared ground around which the thatched huts and houses are clustered; I can identify the granary beside the cooking hut, outside of which are a large rock, a tree, and the wooden bench on which we sat last night. Basic.

I want to cry, but no tears come. That I don't know where

my phone is must be another one of my memory gaps. On the other hand, people do lose stuff without noticing at the time. But the phone is gone, and if nobody's found it, I have no chance. I don't even know where to look for it. I open the door and see Swagga and Jix lounging outside. If we were back home, Swagga would probably give me a nice hug. I need one right now, but it's just not the done thing here. PDA between boys and girls, even husbands and wives, is just not done. If I even hint that Swagga is my boyfriend, that would formalize things and we are as good as engaged to be married.

"What's up?" Swagga asks.

"Have you seen my phone?"

"No, Chanda, not this again. I thought coming here was supposed to help you."

"I know."

"What happened?"

"I could have lost it."

"Well, I guess you did, if you didn't throw it into the bush on purpose."

"Why would I do such a silly thing?"

He shrugs. He could spare me some hope here. As I follow him and Jix, people greet us, and we mumble back good morning left and right. Most faces I remember, but names? Eish.

"You really have a lot of peeps, dude."

In the morning light, I see a woman who is probably in her twenties but somehow looks older. She has a scarf tied haphazardly round her head and her clothes are loose and faded. She is all smiles as she calls out a greeting from where she is washing plates and things by a tap a short distance away from the cooking hut. I'm so relieved when her voice brings back the memory of her the night before.

"I'll bring you some water for washing, it's heating on the fire."

It's Cousin, Amai Roddy. I thank her and ask her about my phone but she hasn't seen it.

Am I making a big deal about nothing? It could be anywhere. Outside in the high grass, somewhere in the homestead. I can't even dial my number and hear my ring-tone since nobody has reception.

I tell the boys, "I think we should head back today. I'm so done with being here. It's too much. And apparently it doesn't help me anyway. No one should have to go through this."

"What's going through this about any of it?" asks Jix, "This is real life. People live like this and it's natural."

"For them, not me. I want to go home. I think I'll be better off in some plush sanatorium in Jo'burg, with nice white walls, clean bedding and clean bathrooms. Rumbi and John will send me there and I'll be fine, maybe I won't be drugged or anything. I'll just see a therapist of some sort."

Swagga has his hands in his pockets. "Dude, I'm with you on going home. No offence, but this place is kind of ratchet. It's cool for the oans who're used to it—props to them, but I'd rather go face my bhally. I'd trade punishment with bore-dom and hardship anytime."

Jix stops and kicks a stone into the grass. "Don't be so quick to go near an institution. You won't like it. At least here you're free to be yourself and think what you like without someone making it something it's not."

"Hmh."

"The car is still bust anyway. If we can fix it, we can talk about departure."

◆ ◆ ◆

By the time Cousin Amai Roddy has served us tea and bread with jam, my equilibrium is restored and I accept my loss. Cousin tells us Sven and Vimbiko have gone with other cousins to bring the car back. They left Jix to sleep, since he had driven all the way here and needed a little extra rest. Cousin doesn't say why they didn't wake up Swagga, but I can guess. He's got that kind of useless look about him, like if you ask him to do something, he'll probably just stuff it up and end up getting in the way. I don't blame them. Swagga is good for town things, like picking you up for parties, paying for drinks, loud-mouthing other guys on your behalf, but not for real-life things. He'd probably be pushing the car with one hand while the other is busy hitching up his pants.

I pinch his cheek and tease him. "Ah shame, bruh, nobody remembered that you're also a big strong man who can get the job done. They left you sleeping with the womenfolk."

He kisses his teeth at me and shrugs me off. Jix and I laugh.

The sun shines on the hill in the West, which seems to be a natural border for the village. Somebody is coming down from there. It's Tete Victoria.

"What was she doing up there?" I ask a kid who collects my empty plate.

"Getting in touch with the spirits," the girl says.

"Uhhhh," says Swagga and I'm embarrassed.

I look up to the top of the little mountain where a red rock stands, and wonder what I would find if I went up there.

When we're done with breakfast, Jix and Swagga head up the path to look for Sven and Vimbiko, and I duck into the kitchen where Tete and Cousin are seated. There's very little of the smoke of last night, as there are now only embers glowing in the pit.

I say my good mornings, and when I sit down and cross my legs on the cowhide on the floor next to Tete, she looks at me as if cataloguing my appearance: hair tied up in the scarf loaned to me by Cousin, my button-down shirt stretched across a modest chest and seriously wrinkled, and blue skinny jeans that feel rather uncomfortable on day two of continuous wear. Cousin had asked me about my European hair—hardly recognizable as such anymore—and said she found it very strange but nice.

Tete Victoria says, "Where did you get those bushy eyebrows that are like chongololos walking across your face?"

Cousin laughs and declares that they must be from my mother's side of the family, because no one on their side is so unlucky.

Yes, well in the last few weeks I have been too busy forgetting things to have the eyebrows threaded and shaped like I usually do. And this is a running joke with my relatives, so haha, tell me a new one.

"But you are light in complexion, like us," Tete Victoria

says. "You're lucky in that respect."

So politically incorrect, oh my gosh!

"You have nice big eyes that see the world clearly, but those big ears of yours are unfortunate."

Eish! Anything else? Sounds like I'm the girl from African Middle Earth.

Cousin is now busy, in and out of the kitchen, putting things away and generally just faffing about. She has a busy air about her, but all she seems to be doing is moving the same things on the wooden dresser that's against the wall.

"You look just like your father's sister, Enia, when she was the same age. She was the most beautiful girl in the village. Maybe you still have time to grow into your looks, and then you will need a kraal for all your suitors."

So rude. But I just smile. What can I say? She's keeping me humble, I guess.

"And your father, John?"

Yes, I know he is called John.

"Where is he? Why has he not come with you?"

"Um, he was at work."

At this she laughs to herself, and takes a pinch of snuff up one nostril.

"Is that right? John." She says nothing for a while.

"John has forgotten where he came from. It's been years since he was last here. He does not visit his father's and mother's graves. He does not come back to see how his family are doing. He does not attend our ceremonies for the ancestors. Not even the annual ones. He is the head of his family. He should be here with you. Instead he lets you come here on your own, with just these young men who are not even your family, not even our folks! A British! A British you bring here."

"A German."

"It's one and the same. It is unseemly and disrespectful."

Minefield. I'm about to open my mouth and confess that my parents didn't let me do anything, that I just left a note for them telling them where I have gone and came here to ask for her help because Tete Frasia instructed me to, when Tete Victoria says, "Regardless, I know why you are here. I was told that you would be coming and I can help you."

I am so relieved. There is something about this old aunty of mine that makes me feel like if anyone would know what my ancestors are trying to tell me by sending my totem animal to me, it would be her. She seems to be connected with the whole, with the spirits, or pretends and piles it on big.

"You are maDube, the hornless one of the plains, manjenjenje, the one to whom praise belongs. Your ancestors have a reason for calling you back here to your home. Don't worry, you will be healed. Just follow my instructions over the next few days and all will be well."

Next few days! This is not ideal. I want her to give me some herbs or something, or do whatever she has to do to make it all better, today, so that I can get back. I can't imagine another night in the company of some rodent, in the hideous discomfort of the only bed in the house. A few days? Oh man, I'm doomed.

"Come back at sunset and I will begin our work," Tete Victoria says and gets up and leaves the kitchen.

Cousin pops into the kitchen and heats more hot water

in a big metal bucket on the fire—my cue to leave. As she pokes about the embers, she says, "Don't you worry, little mother, Tete knows what she is doing. Everyone for miles around comes to her with their problems. She has a gift for healing."

❖ ❖ ❖

I film them pushing the car down the dust road towards me. There's a small crowd of people and lots of noise. The little kids are running up and down, screeching with excitement. Fiso is above it all, trotting along, stopping to sniff at the grass, disappearing then turning up ahead to wait for the crowd. Swagga is at the wheel—of course. It's the best place for him while the rest are pushing wherever they can lay their hands on the car. They're covered in dust when they stop in a clearing under a big tree, just outside the homestead. A big boulder pushes up from the ground here, competing with the tree for height. The little kids clamber up the rock and sit at the top to watch, as if they are in a theatre.

Sven sermonizes in German, which no one understands. He pops the hood open and peers inside.

"Nothing new. It's the paneuser," he says and hammers something inside the hood with a steel bar. "It's always the paneuser with this model. I guess it did its job pretty well since 1982? Looks like the original."

"I guess," Jix shrugs.

"We need a new one. And the right tools, of course."

"Of course," Jix echoes and says to Vimbiko, "We probably can scavenge something here?"

"I don't know," Vimbiko answers. "I will have to check, what is there. But if we need anything, we have to find some way to get to the growth point, which involves a few hours' walk to the main junction and then a twenty-minute ride in whatever vehicle stops to give us a lift. It's the work of at least a day to go and buy anything. Luckily there is a car breaker not far from the growth point, and we should be able to get most of the things we'll need."

I thought it would take a night, the weekend at most, to get the car running, and by Sunday we would be home. It's Saturday today. We are stuck. It may be my kumusha, but that doesn't mean I want to be here for days either.

"Good morning Chanda, how did you sleep?" Vimbiko comes to me with a big smile. He has nice white teeth, a nice smile. He would be quite a beefcake if he wasn't so much of an SRB. I can just imagine trying to go out with him to a club or something. It would be a bust move, he'd be so out of place and then he'd open his mouth and speak in his proper Shona and the oans would just blast. I could groom him, but then he'd have to be the strong silent type—that is, he'd just never speak.

"I slept well if you slept well," I say. At least with everyday greetings it's not so awkward to reply to him in the same manner.

"I slept well."

O-M-freaking-G, he is so uncool. He is wearing a snug red T-shirt today, two sizes too small, easily. On the other hand it shows off some impressive muscle definition. He has on faded khaki shorts and some rubber criss-cross sandals. They look like the type made from car tires. So, bust, definitely not taking him anywhere. He hands me some hard, round, gourd-like thing.

"I brought you a treat."

Ah! I know this fruit, it's a damba, we called it an African orange as kids, but I understand it's known as a klapper apple. Go figure. I really used to like this fruit.

"Thanks." I find myself smiling genuinely.

"Ah, so sweet." Swagga rolls up, "Young love. If I'd known all it took was wild fruit to win your heart, I would have come to the bush a lot sooner and saved all the dough I spent taking you out on dates."

"Whatever."

I don't know why he gets like this. He is talking himself out of my orbit. He grabs the fruit from me and tosses it up in the air. Vimbiko just shakes his head and walks away, and I have to confess that I feel ashamed of Swagga. He catches the orange and leans over to sneak a kiss.

"Forget it." I punch him in the arm and the fruit falls on the ground and cracks open.

"Why did you do that?"

"Think about it."

Jix comes up and says, "Ah, young love. Ever filled with broken oranges."

Swagga glares at him, I glare at Swagga, and Sven steps up and says, "You guys all right? I sense some vibes here. Come on, be friends."

But I'm annoyed and confused. I had wanted to ask Vimbiko to record a segment for my video and now he's disappeared. Sometimes I think Swagga and I should just quit and be friends only. I'm never sure with him whether we're really in love or just hanging out because we get each other in a very laid-back kind of way. It's easy being with him, maybe too easy.

I leave the guys and walk to the house to find Vimbiko. He's not there. I ask Cousin where Vimbiko has gone, and she, busy as always, shrugs and says, "Where he always goes."

I want to ask her how Vimbiko is related to me, but she bustles off with buckets of water and dirty clothes in a canvas bag. I slink off back to where Swagga and Jix are chilling under the tree, while Sven is busy tinkering away with the car's engine.

The little kids are now busy herding the goats with sticks, creating more noise than movement. I take out my camera and film them, but my heart isn't in it. I'm feeling restless. I don't want to hang out with Swagga anymore. He should be sensitive about people here, even more than Sven, who is from Germany. And really! That stunt of trying to kiss me in front of people. Was he for real with that? I feel like I would like some time alone. I walk away. Swagga knows I'm pissed off and he's in some weird mood that will only make things worse.

❖ ❖ ❖

Surely if I stay close to where I can see people all the time I'll be fine. I could get to the river behind the homestead by staying in sight of other homesteads all the while. If it gets too bushy, I can always turn around. My heart is pounding as I make my way down the path to the left of Tete Victoria's kitchen. It's a pretty open area, and there are huts and houses all along the path. Here and there people call out a greeting and a couple insist on stopping me for a chat and introducing themselves. Apparently they are all somehow related to me. The Tiregeyis appear to be a very big clan and they all seem to know John and ask me when he will come back to see them.

I'm glad that Cousin lent me a headscarf and a wrap-around so that I don't stand out too much in my jeans. None of the women are wearing trousers. It's the beginning of the hot season and everything is still dry and brown from the winter, but the sun is pretty strong. I like hot weather. Rumbi is always telling me to wear a hat and cover up so I won't get dark, but I like it when my skin goes a deep brown. It makes me feel more there somehow. It's crazy, I know, but it's a more real colour than just a very light brown.

There's a gentle breeze and the sky is so blue. I feel happy. There are thorny shrubs here and there, and no signs of Sekuru baboon and his cohorts. And I'm glad I've taken this time away from Swagga. I actually remember now that before all the trouble with my memory started I had begun to feel like that spark was gone between us—what made me smile and feel warm inside every time I saw him. It was nice then, so much fun. The affection was natural and heart-felt, and when he called me dude, it was sweet and special and we were always laughing about stuff. I'm thinking that without my blackout and memory loss, without the condition, we probably would have split by now. You don't split at a time like that, it's not cool, so you duke it out and hold together. I admire him for that, but anytime longer is time wasted, and nobody knows how much time they have. If we break up now, we'll probably stay friends. I think Swagga is feeling the same way but he won't say it. He'll bounce back quickly enough, he's got a whole bunch of friends, who call themselves the BDP crew—Boogie Down Productions. And with all the other girls waiting in the wings, he'll have a new chick in no time. That thought kinda makes me sick. Even though I don't want him as my boyfriend anymore, I still want to be important in his life. What if his next chick is much cooler than me and I'm relegated to his past? I won't like it, but I may have to just accept it. I'm an honorary member of the BDP crew and I wonder if that will change too. Those guys are crazy. It would have been hell if he'd brought even one more of his boys with him. Jix is a bit strange but I can handle him. The rest of them are just out of control. I'm sure Tete Victoria would have chased them away by now.

◆◆◆

"Did you see mermaids down by the river?" It's the little kid with the runny nose.

Now I don't want to paint a stereotypical picture of little village kids, but there's no escaping the fact that this little kid needs to pick the dried snot off his nose. He's cute and all, but eish! I almost want to do it for him myself. Earlier, when I took my camera and filmed the kids dancing to "Via Orlando" that Jix played for them on his phone, I tried to clean this little boy's nose with a tissue, but he yelled and they all ran away laughing. Now he's back, standing a good distance away, asking me about mermaids.

"No," I tell him.

When the kids aren't hanging around parading themselves, they are clamouring around Sven, who is still working on the Peugeot. I'm sure he'll experience a lot of this on his travels around the country and down South. At first the kids would sneak up, touch him, and run away, but now they are hovering around, taking turns to hold onto his hand.

My little friend asks me, "Are you also white?"

"No!" I'm dumbfounded. How? I guess everyone here is well and truly toasted by the sun, but really! Maybe the weave on my head is what confused them, and right now I am super paranoid that something may have dug itself in there and built a nest. I've heard such horror stories. I kind of want to remove it. Nobody here will care what my hair looks like anyway.

I know Swagga will draw the line at combing through my weave section by section to make sure nothing is hiding there from last night. Anyway, I'm still not feeling him. Maybe later I will ask Cousin to do it.

◆ ◆ ◆

In the meantime, it's sunset and time for my appointment with Tete Victoria. There were no incidents all day. No black spots in my memory, no zebra sightings. My trip to the river was nice and peaceful and I just sat there in a shady spot and listened to the water bouncing and bubbling over the rocks. I felt calm and happy.

Tete is not in the kitchen but in another hut, a squarish one. I leave my sneakers outside as I've been instructed.

This hut is smaller than the kitchen and there are clay pots and bits and bobs everywhere. In the middle is a firepit like in the kitchen and there is something with a strong smell burning in the embers.

"Drink this," Tete says, when I sit down on the floor opposite her and cross my legs.

I probably shouldn't, I think. The whole room feels very hocus-pocus to me, and I'm not sure I should be involving myself in this kind of stuff. Maybe Rumbi and John are right to denounce it all, but in all my seventeen years, I have never believed that Tete Frasia would let me do anything that would harm me. Many strange things took place when I was a child, and she would tell my parents to leave me out of them. There was a time when some serious stuff was going down in the family, like when Rumbi and John became born again, and whenever relatives visited us, Tete Frasia would tell me to stay in my room. And now, even though Tete Victoria is a bit rude, I don't feel uneasy around her.

I take the drinking gourd she hands me and take a sip of the warm brew. It is so bitter I almost gag. It tastes like someone has ground a whole lot of quinine tablets and made a tea from it.

"Drink it all," Tete says, pushing the gourd back up to my mouth, forcing the stuff down my throat. I'm sure the face I make is cartoon-worthy. I use every muscle when I grimace, and my tongue feels like it just fell out.

"Keep it down," she says rather forcefully, so for fear of unknown consequences I force myself to calm my reflexes. Some people just have that authority. Tete grumbles under her breath and then begins clapping her palms together and saying things that I cannot understand. Here and there I catch phrases like "those who are in the spirit." Uh-oh, I think, this is the ancestor stuff that John and Rumbi are always preaching about, and even though I don't usually listen to them I'm beginning to feel a bit uneasy. I am out of my depth here. My parents are always preaching against spiritual and ancestral ties, what have I got myself into? I should just say, "Thanks, Tete, I've changed my mind." She throws some twigs and leaves onto the embers, and with a great hissing, crackling, and sparking, smoke rises—quite dramatically I must say—and a pungent odour fills the room. It's not entirely unpleasant, but it's strong and smells very green. It eventually tickles my nose, really violently, and I start sneezing uncontrollably. I sneeze and sneeze and sneeze and the next thing I know I am opening my eyes to find myself lying on my side, on the cowhide, on the floor.

◆◆◆

I don't know how long I have been there or what happened after the sneezing, but there is no smoke in the hut anymore, not even the smell lingers. Tete Victoria is sitting before me, pinching snuff into her nose and staring into the dying embers. "You can go now," she says.

I have questions, but my tongue feels all twisted up and can't seem to form words. It's too much effort to try, so I just haul myself up and make to leave. It's not so easy, because I feel strange and light-headed, as if my body were floating. I launch forward, aiming for the open doorway, holding onto it to keep myself from pitching forward and down onto the dusty ground outside.

My legs feel like rubber and I can hear my heart pounding in my ears. It's dark outside. What did she make me inhale and how long have I been out? The kids are still playing, dogs are barking, and people are moving around, but I feel like I am far away from it all.

"Hey, Chanda, I kept a drumstick for you. Your Tete hooked us up lekker. She killed a rooster for us. Come and get it before Jix takes it," Swagga says.

"Hahaaaa!" Jix is killing himself laughing. "Since when, Swagga? Check it out, Chanda, oan is trying to get some game on. He got scooped by the village Romeo and now he's trying to one-up him."

"Shut up, Jix, it's not like that, bruh. That oan's got no game, with his bust rural lyrics and wild fruit. Me and Chanda go way back and . . . "

"Whatever, man!"

It's a full moon like in Harare when the power's gone. Vimbiko is sitting with the other cousins on the veranda outside the brick house. I know he can hear them where they are, on the flat rock outside the kitchen, which is our eating area and general hang-out. Does he even speak English—well, the kind that we speak at any rate. I don't know. I hope he doesn't understand what they're talking about. I can hear Swagga saying something not nice. I want to tell him to stop being childish, but it's just too much effort. I need to go lie down.

"Ey, Chanda, what's up with you?" Swagga is waving a hand in front of my eyes.

"Hmm?"

I really need to lie down.

"Yo, Chanda is smoked. Maybe we need to get some of whatever she's been given."

"Jix, you've had enough shit in your system to last a lifetime. Go and finish eating your chicken, man." Swagga takes me by the arm. "Come and sit down, dude, you look wasted."

"I think you should lie down." Sven puts in his two cents, then asks Swagga, "Did you say *lekker* before? Does that mean tasty?"

"Yep."

"Aha, we say the same in German, lecker. I can remember that . . . "

Cousin comes bustling out of the kitchen.

"Oh, good lord," she says. "Chanda, come with me. You need to go straight to bed. What can amai be thinking letting you wander around like this right now?"

I smell her smoky, slightly sweaty scent as she wrests me from Swagga and leads me up the small incline to my bedroom.

"Vimbiko, come and help me here," she calls.

He is strong and solid, unlike Swagga, who is lean and kind of all over the place. Vimbiko must have just bathed because I smell soap on his skin and, surprisingly enough, body lotion. He strikes me as a Vaseline petroleum jelly kind of guy—basic and functional. He even seems to have used some kind of cologne or antiperspirant with a citrusy smell. Or am I hallucinating?

Oh the bed! The hole in the mattress—a place to stick

my bum. And suddenly it's really funny and I'm giggling as they lay me down. I want to tell them about the order of the blankets so that I am not covered by the one I don't like that's got all the balled-up bits of lint on it and has a musty smell, but I have no way of forming the words and even as my head hits the pillow I feel like I'm falling bum first through the hole in the mattress into a deep pit and then it's all dark.

I half-awake several times during the night to all sorts of weird dreams about rural life and the past and the present. I see that there is a light in the room with me. Vimbiko by my bed.

IT'S A WHOLE OTHER WORLD: THE ESCAPE

Everything seems extra clear when I wake up. Colours shine bright and the sounds are sharp like crystal—the birds, feet on the ground, voices, and I know where I am.

I'm feeling a bit panicky, though. I'm not aware what Tete did or what she was saying with her chanting and to whom. What if she's making some sacrifices and covenants on my behalf for which I will later have to repay? It's a whole other world here and what may seem normal and reasonable to her may not be so to me. She's the one who deals with ancestors and stuff, I don't know anything about it. There is always a dark side to those things. Maybe there's a reason Rumbi and John have taken the stance they have. I don't know these relatives of mine, but my parents are my parents, and even if I don't agree with everything they believe, that doesn't mean it's not valid. John would know more about his family. Why doesn't he want to have anything to do with them? Maybe I have been foolish, putting myself in the hands of people who wish us harm.

I try to act very casual and normal when I meet up with Swagga and Jix, who are outside brushing their teeth. Swagga offers me a tin cup with water for rinsing, saying,

"Dude, you were out of it last night. What happened?"

"Eish bruh, some weird shit on a fire, smoke and stuff. I'll tell you later."

"You missed out on the gwaans last night," Jix says and puts his empty cup on the window ledge.

"What gwaans? What happened?"

"Apparently, like somewhere just beyond the hill nearest to us, a lion got someone's goat and they said they could hear it all night making that lowing sound lions make."

"A lion? Sure."

"I tell you, a lion, bruh! Someone even saw it."

"Stop playing."

"I'm serious, dude, ask Sven."

"Please Swagga . . . Sven doesn't speak Shona. He isn't a good witness. You probably translated some tall tale for him to spread. I know you."

"He's not lying, Chanda," Jix says. "We were just thinking that maybe we should leave this place sooner rather than later. I mean, we have to make a plan about the car anyway. We talked to one of the older guys from next door, he's got a donkey cart and he says he'll be going to the shops. Swagga and I were thinking maybe we can go and either catch a bus back into town and send someone back for the car, or if we find the parts we need at the growth point, we send back the parts."

"And who will fix the car?"

"Sven. He said so, even promised. He seems to like it here and I'm sure he'll stay."

"No, I don't think so," says Sven.

We hadn't heard him approach. "I am not so keen to

be around hungry lions. In the news it's always the dumb foreigner who gets eaten."

"Dude!" Jix packs out laughing, "Just like how in the movies when you see a black oan, you just know he's going to be the first to die. Makes it even between us, bruh."

The boys crack up.

Swagga addresses me when he's stopped laughing. "I know . . . you came here to be helped . . . with your issues, but I think we have to be sensible here."

I'm not about to argue. I'm in agreement. Not because of the lion or anything, simply because I'm beginning to doubt the wisdom of having come here in the first place. Yesterday just freaked me out and I'm ready to get outta here. This traditional healing stuff is too far out there for me.

❖ ❖ ❖

We don't really say goodbye. We tell Cousin we're going in the donkey cart to catch a ride to the shops to look for the things we need for the car. Tete Victoria and Vimbiko are nowhere to be found. And thank goodness our luggage is not big and bulky. The donkey cart is just something else, but we all fit inside. The guys dangle their legs over the edge at the back.

The kids run a little way behind us, cheering and laughing for a while, then fall back when it gets boring because the pace is so slow. I still have some battery left on the vidcam—the last of my spare one and I film the waving kids, the receding homestead, and the people who greet us along the way.

It's slow and dusty, but quite fun, memorable for sure.

I feel a bit like a kid again, doing crazy, impulsive things. We joke around a lot. Sven feels very much like part of the group. None of us have actually managed to have a proper wash since we got here but we have somehow managed. The bathroom in the house was so unused it was too much effort to try and clean it. It seems everyone just used the bathing shacks to the left of the toilets—two straw-walled cubicles built around a flat rock. You just took your bucket in there and you washed.

◆ ◆ ◆

The sky stretches blue into forever and the sun shines high yellow. Swagga has got his shades on as usual and is singing, "In the club, in the club . . . with my shades on." Jix has found a way to lie on his back and is watching the sky. Occasionally he makes some remark about being free from the machine. "The matrix has us," he keeps saying, "we are free out here. Why go back?"

I'm not sure we are leaving because of the lion. I think here we are just too out of our element. It seemed like a big adventure when we started, but when reality bites, it can all get too much. Sven, I'm not sure what his story is, he's been spending a lot of time staring at me when he thinks I'm not looking. I don't know what's happening with these guys. Maybe it's just a competition thing. I mean, right now he is smiling at me warmly, his blue eyes crinkling at the corners.

"Hey Chanda. What are you going to do after the summer?"

"I don't know. And you?"

"I have a trainee position in a garage lined up. But I don't know either. We could not know together?"

Ee? What's happening here? I can't suddenly have become too cute to resist overnight. Did Tete give me some kind of love potion or something? As Rumbi would say, when she is baffled beyond hope, "I can't understand." Under my breath I always add, "it." When I think of it now, it makes me laugh.

Swagga stakes his claim again, "Ah, watch it, bruh!"

I try to iron out the tension, "You are not sure about your trainee gig anymore?"

"It just seems so . . . real. I mean, cars, motors . . . All logic, no life."

Jix snaps his finger and points at him. "Yes."

The light of the sun around Sven's blond hair creates a thin halo. I wonder if he ever had long hair, and to lift his mood I ask him, "Did you ever have long hair?"

"No," he says, sounding insulted.

"You should."

"Why?"

"Every man should have long hair at least once in his life. Before it's all gone."

He wants to say something, but Swagga is faster, with, "Forget the hair, that's girl stuff, think of the dough, the money, bruh. Auto mechanic, man, you will make big money, you will build the next BMW, imagine!"

"I don't think so. I will work in a garage fixing cars, which are nowadays built to break in the first place, for people that are in a bad mood because they work hard so they can afford that car of their dreams . . . well, not of their dreams . . . Ah, what do I know?"

"Dude, you're my kind of human," Jix says and they fist-bump.

Sven seems more caught up in the middle of everyday life than we are. We are all from well off families not worried about money. We pretty much get everything we want from our parents, always did. Sven is like Vimbiko, taking his life into his own hands already.

It's almost like my thoughts shift something in the matrix. Suddenly there's an almighty jolt, as though we've been hit by an elephant, and we all tumble out of the cart as it falls sideways and then we are lying in the dirt checking our bones and joints and scratches. Luckily nobody has any major injuries.

"Oh shame!" says VaTombo, the driver of the cart. Somehow he's managed to land on his feet and has taken off his floppy hat to scratch his head in wonder. "The wheel came off."

Of course it did. This is just the kind of luck we've been having all along. The two donkeys stand there knowing that it's not their problem, chewing on God-knows-what and shaking their heads. It must be so uncomplicated to be a donkey.

Sven is already on his knees inspecting the cart and cries out, "It's worse, it's not the wheel, it's the axle, it's completely rusted through and broke off where it is . . . was . . . connected to the wheel."

"I was hoping to reach Saratoga before it broke. I was going there to get it fixed. Carrying four extra people was too much," says the driver.

Great. I don't know why he didn't tell us at the start. Now we are stuck in the middle of nowhere. If I didn't know better, I would say that we are in exactly the same place we were when we were lost before and Jix got all crunk. It's tall grass and trees and overgrown paths.

Swagga kicks his rucksack in disgust.

"This is getting to be a habit," Sven says, getting up and clapping the dirt off his hands. He seems to be finding this situation funny. "I cannot believe this. We are the unluckiest bastards ever. It must be you guys." He is full out laughing now and his face has gone red.

I'm glad he's so amused. I am not. We are screwed. I don't need to know much about this place to know that any walk will surely kill us.

Saratoga is the growth point where we were hoping to catch a bus. I really don't know if Sven means to travel back to Harare with us, he just said he wasn't going to stay at the village without us, or perhaps he just means to continue somewhere else once we reach civilization again. He is the drifter-dude. Jix is looking up at the sky, arms spread wide and turning around in a slow circle as if receiving a message from Heaven. He starts to laugh and delivers a sermon. "You see how insignificant we are? As ants, right now. Nature is all-powerful and in the end, it will win. We think we have all the answers, but we are here by the grace of some entity that is laughing at us right now. Who do we think we are?" He shouts out the last bit.

I think he's becoming hysterical. It must be all this nature or maybe he ate a worm too many.

"Yo chill, bruh! This is bush, we don't need to call

attention to ourselves." Swagga gives Jix a meaningful look and I'm reminded of Sekuru Gudo and the roaming lion.

This is worse than I thought.

"So. What shall we do?" Good Samaritan VaTombo is still scratching his head as if this whole thing is the biggest mystery, like he didn't know there was a chance this could happen. A broken axle on a donkey cart that most likely was first used to help build the pyramids. Tjo!

He says, "There are two donkeys and five people. Who will come with me on the other one? I can go for help, my cousin lives over the hill. He will lend me his cart."

There is no question about it. If all of us can't go, then all of us stay. We're not even going to have that discussion.

"Oans, we are screwed big time," Swagga says.

"Can we walk to Saratoga?" I ask VaTombo.

"Ahhh, it's a bit of a walk and the way I came it will be very complicated if you don't know the way."

"Okay, how about walking back to the homestead?"

"Yeaaahhh. You can walk." But his expression says he doubts it.

What does he expect us to do? I ask him, "What would be the best thing to do?"

"You can wait for me here by the cart. I will be back." We agree, and he confirms he'll be back before evening.

But he takes both donkeys and I'm not sure how this will work. Why take both donkeys? This dude is shady. I don't think he is being very straightforward with us. There is a good chance VaTombo is not coming back. Why come back for something you couldn't sell to me as firewood?

◆◆◆

The thing is, if we hadn't waited forever for that guy, we probably would have made it back to the homestead. As it is, by the time we decide to try and make our way back, it's already late in the day. At some cluster of huts where we stop to ask for directions, a guy playing tsoro with his friends offers to take us to the Tiregeyis. I can't explain to you the confusion we suffered when we arrived there. Sure, their name is Tiregeyi, but these are not my relatives. It is not the place where we spent the last two days! We can ask to stay overnight, but the people and the place just give off a dark vibe—and in the bush your gut feeling can decide your fate.

We part ways with our guide, because quite frankly we don't think he knows the people we are talking about at all, but is simply fascinated by the presence of Sven, who is looking around like a five-year-old in Disneyland. And so we are nowhere. There is a dry river bed where the ground is cracked clay and little black insects are scurrying in and out of crevices. I know about these ants, they're called mamatsu and sting like crazy. Behind us are long brown grass, a couple of large trees, some anthills, and lots of little dry green bushes. It's late afternoon, and the temperature has started to drop, though we are still hot and sweaty from tramping around helplessly all freaking day.

Jix speaks out in frustration, "Why are we so lost? There are the hills, we need to walk in this exact direction to get to the homestead, but we are just not getting there." If he had a hat on, Jix would throw it to the ground. Swagga has opted for throwing himself into the long grass, against the trunk of a big tree. On the other side of the tree, a little distance away, is a huge anthill. I could swear I have been here before, but it was probably an hour ago when we passed here.

Throughout our march we have randomly stopped to check for a signal on our phones. Even if there had been a signal, whom would we have called? I never knew it could be possible in this day and age, but it is—we are properly lost.

"Dude, you should have never got in our car," Jix says to Sven, standing with his hands on his hips and shaking his head.

"Oh, but this is real life," Sven says. "Now when I go home I can tell everyone what an adventure I had in the bush with you guys and some donkeys and all because of a French car."

"If you get back home," Jix says, throwing himself down next to Swagga beside the tree. "Whatever bag of bones they'll fly home if they find you out here at all."

"I don't know if I want to hear that right now."

"Did you know that long ago they didn't bury the dead, they would just throw them onto anthills and the ants would take care of the bodies? I'm sure if you open that one over there and dig, you'll probably find human bones at the bottom of it. Efficient, don't you think?"

No one replies.

Jix just can't shut up about nature reclaiming the world. "Human beings were created to work towards the destruction of the earth for its eventual regeneration. We are just cogs in the wheel and one day, the machine will stop."

"Do you think people out here will be the survivors then?" Sven asks. "Because it seems to me like out here, there is no machine working, not even rusty axles."

"In years to come, there won't be any of these untouched spaces anymore. If a third world war breaks out and oans start blasting chemical weapons. It's going to be end times. We might as well sit back and enjoy God's green earth while we can."

"And become some lion's dinner before the night is over," Swagga says.

He is actually smiling. I don't think this is funny. It's getting dark and we have no plan. I am just grateful that we haven't come across any baboons.

"What are we going to do?" I ask.

In the end, we sit by the tree and eat the last of Jix's biltongs, share a warm Coke that Sven finds in his backpack and some chewing gum that was in the pocket of my hoodie.

❖ ❖ ❖

All this time I have been half-expecting Vimbiko to turn up and rescue us again. It's properly dark now and no one has come. Meanwhile Sven is starting a fire under the big tree.

"Can you imagine this?" Jix is crouched down, holding out his palms to the flames, which are slowly catching hold. "Between us we have at least three hundred dollars. But what good is money out here, right now?"

"And a couple of credit cards, I bet," throws in Sven.

"What do you say, bruh?" Jix turns to Swagga, who has folded himself in.

"I don't want to talk about that. This is just bullshit."

Jix takes no note of Swagga's attitude. Neither do I, we know Swagga gets this way, sulking to himself when he can't deal with things.

"This is what I keep saying, guys," says Jix. "The life we are living is not real. It's all an illusion created by the grand masters to keep humanity docile. If we all refuse to feed the machine, it will stop, and when it stops, we have the chance to save ourselves."

"What machine are you talking about?" I ask. He pretends not to hear me. "What about the purpose of humans to work towards the eventual regeneration of the earth. I thought you said this was our destiny?"

This conversation is making my brain hurt. I am more concerned by the reality of our current situation. These guys seem to have forgotten about the lion hanging about in this area munching on people's goats. Not to mention all the other bush citizens lurking in the dark. And the eerie shadows the fire casts everywhere.

"I really miss Rumbi and John. I wish they were here."

"I've been thinking this all day. If they were, then I wouldn't be here," Swagga replies. "I would probably be chilling right now with my crew."

"I'm your crew. I'm here," Jix says and claps his hands. I think Jix is actually enjoying every bit of this.

"I thought, Chanda, that in your culture it is disrespectful to say your parents' given names. Why do you do this?" Sven asks.

"She thinks she's being cool and rebellious," Swagga answers. He is now leaning against the tree trunk, legs stretched out. And he's lowered his sunglasses over his eyes again. I wonder if he thinks he might magically find himself in the club just by doing that. But I think he's just trying to hide from reality.

"It's a very small rebellion," Sven says.

"Well, in our culture, it's a big deal . . . and it's fun. The way they behave sometimes, I feel like they're more John and Rumbi and not Baba and Mama. They seem very much like two people making it up as they go along."

"So you are saying that, in fact, you do not respect them?"

Eish! This Sven is hard work, with all his interest in our ways. He is one of those deep listeners, unlike Swagga.

"I just don't understand them, that's all, and it's easier for me in my head if I just think of them as regular people."

"But they are regular people," Sven persists.

Behind me I hear Swagga's snort. He's laughing at me. Jix is lying close to the crackling fire, hands behind his head, looking up at the stars. No help there.

"Yes, but they aren't supposed to be. Here, you respect your parents no matter what. You listen to them even when they are wrong. You are not supposed to talk back, you are supposed to do what they say. They are not regular people, they are your boss, they are your everything."

"But soon you are eighteen and you can be independent pretty much after . . . " There's a twitch in his eyes, and he continues. "I am now nineteen and I have been independent since . . . hmmh . . . I guess . . . since I was sixteen. I saved money for this trip. I don't always listen to my parents and I say so when I don't agree and they must also take into consideration how I feel. Surely if you are just calm and

113

reasonable when you speak to them they listen to you."

Actually, I know that John and Rumbi are not so bad. I know kids with stricter parents who are very old-fashioned. I'm starting to feel bad for giving a bad impression of them. They don't deserve that. It's just that they don't seem very grounded in real life. I think praying and stuff is all very well, but it cannot be the only thing.

"All right, they're not so bad," I say, just to end the conversation.

Sven starts again, "But you—"

At this, Swagga bursts out laughing. "Bruh, you're one tough oan. Give it a rest, man. We all know Chanda needs therapy, but if you keep up with this, she's going to poke a stick in your eye."

I swat his feet, but I'm glad he saved me. Even though we can really annoy each other, Swagga's always got my back.

Sven says, "So now I keep my thoughts to myself." He smiles and thankfully drops the subject.

Eish!

My irritation with him disappears when he produces a tin of baked beans with a spoon and a big bar of chocolate.

"Emergency rations. I thought to hold onto them, but I think this qualifies, no?"

Everybody gets up. "Yes," we say in a chorus.

It's way past the hour when it would still have been reasonable to hope for rescue. We are over our fear of what might find us out here, and we have made ourselves comfortable around the fire. Again, the sky's crazy with stars. I lean back against Swagga, he puts his arms around me and kisses the side of my neck. I know he's saying sorry for everything, and in this manner, it's all okay. We'll deal with our relationship later. We're all quiet, listening to the call of the crickets, the rustling of small things in the long grass, the soft sighs of the leaves, and for once it feels like peace.

◆◆◆

This all changes when we hear a sound that none of us can fool ourselves into thinking is a cow or a donkey. I have heard it before on *Animal Planet*. Deep, booming grunts from the throat of a lion. Jix and Swagga sit up and look at each other.

"Everything alr—" Sven begins and we shush him. He doesn't know. The lions obviously don't roll like this in his zoo in Germany.

I clue him in: "A lion."

And the rest of Sven's colour leaves his face. We are all holding our breaths, so as not to betray our presence if we let go. I don't know how long we sit there like that, alert and listening, terrified. We don't hear the sound again, but we know our situation has changed. We all stand up and grab our things. We look at the tree.

"It's a big enough tree. I think we can all find some place to put ourselves for the night," I say, "plus it's easy enough to climb."

"If we can climb this tree, bruh, a lion can climb this tree," Jix says, eyeing it dubiously.

Swagga has put his sunglasses away, which indicates that he is in serious mode now.

"I take my chances in the tree," Sven says, already hoisting himself up.

Lucky bastard, going up first, he manages to secure himself the nicest spot. Highest up the tree, with his back supported by a forked branch, he'll be able to comfortably watch the lion munching away on us Zimbos underneath. That's what I call African hospitality! No tourist should ever complain. At the bottom, where the tree forks, there is a hollow where he has left his big rucksack. We leave our bags on top of it as we go up.

"Chanda, if you like, I can share this space. There is room enough for two," says Sven.

He must have read my mind. Or did I look at him too desperately? Of course, I could find somewhere else, but the bottom line is, it is nowhere nearly as comfortable as the space Sven has found. And my personal hospitality ends somewhere.

"If Chanda doesn't take it, I will," Swagga says behind me. "Hurry up and get up the damn tree." He pushes my butt up with his head. I want to laugh because I know he sees himself in the line of fire and he's not happy about it at all.

"Are you scared you're going to get chowed while trying to climb up? Maybe the lion just wants to kiss your nice little buns . . . " My nerves are speaking.

Sven is saying, "I rather share it with Chanda, she is lighter."

"Haha, Chanda, you have suddenly become the flavour of the month," Jix calls out across from where I can see him tying himself to a branch with a rope.

"Where did you get the rope?" I ask.

"From my bag."

"How do you have rope in your bag, just like that?"

"Dude, climb the fuck up!" Swagga is losing his cool.

"Hey, I saw something moving . . . in the shadow behind you!"

Swagga hears the humour in my voice. "Not funny, Chanda, not funny."

It's not as bad as I thought it would be, curled against Sven with my back to his chest. It feels comforting to be this close to someone right now. There are so many things I'm scared of discovering in the tree right now. I can hear a rustling above us that has nothing to do with the other two guys, who are cursing from time to time and complaining.

"Don't worry, it's just birds," Sven says. He seems entirely happy with the situation, his arm around my waist. I won't complain though, because it's making me feel kind of safe.

"But of course, if it is a snake then I am dead, that's all."

"Don't even joke like that, bruh," Jix says. "Yo Swagga, howzit where you are?"

"I don't want to talk to anyone right now. All of you just shut up and leave me alone."

He's on the lowest branches and he's somehow managed to lie flat across two fat ones that are intertwined and pulled together by a vine of some sort, almost like a nest. I hope he doesn't have any company in the dense foliage under him. Swagga is kind of delicate, he would never recover from the trauma.

Our nerves are stretched to the limit and we are all imagining the worst kinds of scenarios.

Sven asks, "What about the baboons?"

"What about them?" I ask.

"Can they climb?"

Jix's high-pitched voice replies. "What do you think monkeys are known for? Their swimming skills? What kinda zoos do you have in Germany? Are you sure it was a zoo? Or was it a circus?"

There is hysterical laughter all around. Leaves rustle against each other. Then we fall quiet again. It's just been too much every day since we left the city.

I had nails when I left H. Nice silk French tips, and now I have three left, the rest all looking like a plumber's. Strangely, I am not bothered by this. When you weigh falling out of a tree into the waiting jaws of a lion against the loss of seven artificial nails, you come to a new understanding of what is important in life. I don't even care that Sven seems far too happy with our arrangement, I am focused on being alive come morning.

When I am almost asleep the low bellows come again and there is a rustling in the grass, but the sounds came from far off. I don't dare breathe. It appears the guys are actually sleeping. Sven's arm is lax and his hand is resting in my lap. I almost want to pull it back around me. My one leg is tingling uncomfortably with pins and needles and my heart is jumping so hard in my chest that it might come tumbling out of my mouth.

There is something moving around in the grass under the tree. Definitely. There's no question of it now because I hear a kind of snorting. A shiver runs down my spine.

Should I warn Swagga? My voice could provoke the lion to act. If I don't say anything the lion could snatch him and I didn't warn him. A lose-lose situation. I choose silence, my fingers feeling my new necklace, its slick surface. Minutes pass and nothing tries to climb up the tree. I risk leaning forward to peep down through the leaves. If something is going to eat us alive I want at least to know what it is.

It's the strangest thing. I see the shimmering white first and feel the heat rising from many bodies in one place and I smell them, too, them and the dead fireplace. The smell of the zebras is so strong in my nose, I can almost taste it on my tongue—earthy, outdoor-animal scent.

Maybe I'm asleep and having one of those dreams that start with you thinking you have woken up, but I have seen this before when I am wide awake and I know. It's not just the one zebra, but a whole herd of them sitting around the tree, facing outwards as if keeping watch. A wreath of zebras—manjenjenje, like our totem praise poem—beautifully adorned, of dazzling beauty. Their striped coats shimmer in the moonlight and I am dazzled by the sight. For the first time all month, zebra-spotting does not fill me with dread.

I want to wake Sven up so he can see them, but the part of me that has always not been sure if I am really seeing a zebra or just imagining it keeps me quiet. Whichever it is, my mind or my eyes deceiving me, it makes me feel safer than I have felt since I drank Tete Victoria's funny tea. Even though a whole herd of zebras may be just the thing to bring the lion to us, all I can think is that it's okay, we're safe.

A LION, ZEBRAS, AND THE PARENTS

We wake up when Swagga falls to the ground. Luckily, he was nearest to the ground. After we see that he is okay, we all have a big laugh at his expense. He swears at us, grabs his bag from the tree, and stalks off.

"Wrong direction!" I call out.

"So?" But he stops and waits until we are all ready.

The morning air is fresh and at the sight of the flattened grass around the tree, a sense of comfort arises in me. I didn't imagine it. The zebras really were there. I keep this to myself. I feel relieved and happy again. We agree about feeling hungry and thirsty, but at the moment there isn't anything we can do about it, we can only decide which direction to walk. At least the hills and rocks in the morning light seem to give us a better idea than yesterday, when the shadows grew longer and longer. For our protection we take big sticks to use as canes to defend ourselves against lions and baboons. Nobody says out loud what everybody is thinking: that the sticks will serve the lion as toothpicks after having feasted on us. Nevertheless, it feels better to have them. And so we march through the high grass with our crooked canes.

Of course the boys don't find a signal for their phones, and mine has mysteriously long gone, but we do find the main dirt road leading to Gumindoga. And in the distance coming towards us is a cloud of dust raised by a car.

We stand by the road as though waiting for a bus, watching silently as the car emerges from the cloud. Before it even reaches us, I know that it is Rumbi and John.

"Do you see what I see?" asks Swagga, who knows our Toyota Land Cruiser.

"Yes."

"How can that be?"

"I guess it just can."

"No way," Jix says.

"What?" asks Sven.

"It's her parents' car," Swagga tells him.

"Wh . . ." Sven looks at me.

Swagga grabs at his forehead dramatically. "We're in a movie, guys, I swear."

"I wish."

"Nobody will believe me if I tell them at home," Sven says in disbelief.

"Welcome to Africa," replies Jix.

The car slows down and behind the dirty window I see my mother and father.

❖ ❖ ❖

Both my parents hug me. I know I think they are a little off track with their hallelujah ways, but when you are lost and not sure that you have done the right thing at all, and you've had to spend days in the company of boys and strange new people, not to say lions, zebras, and baboons, it is always nice to be presented with the folks you know and love best.

I'm expecting a big lecture from them, especially from John, but he says nothing and Mama says, "Chanda, we have been so worried."

"I was fine. You found my letter?"

"Yes."

"We've been having an adventure and we were on our way home today."

"On foot?" She sounds rightly incredulous.

"His car broke down."

"Come on, get in," says my father, eyeing Sven, who introduces himself so respectfully, it's as if he's laying the groundwork to ask for my hand.

I whisper to my mother, "How did you make him come out here?"

"Let's say, we had a talk."

And that is that.

As we drive back to the village, John says, "We read in the newspaper that there was a pride of lions in the area. They dispatched rangers last week to try and hunt them down, but so far they have not managed to find them."

Tell me about it.

"Two people have been taken so far."

"Oh snap! By the lions?" Swagga normally keeps quiet around my parents, but I think he is sufficiently alarmed to forget his usual hesitation.

"They think it's an old lioness that can no longer hunt, and she is preying on humans because they're not so fast.

She's not alone and they're afraid that she is teaching the younger of the pride to hunt this way. Imagine! A whole breed of man-eaters."

"When Tete Frasia told us where you had gone, we panicked after reading that article," Mama says.

"Well, as you can see, we are all fine."

She turns towards Swagga. "Zwagendaba, your parents were looking for you. We naturally assumed that you were with Chanda and assured them you were fine and we'd look for you."

"Thank you."

It seems nobody asked after Jix.

Rumbi and John tell him they are glad to also find him in one piece. His parents probably also spoke to Swagga's parents.

When John talks to Sven, he is all jovial and "Oh is that right?" and "Very pleased to meet you, enjoy our country."

Rumbi only smiles at him and says, "Nice to meet you."

I'm sure we smell rather unfresh, but it's okay around parents. They may wrinkle their noses a bit like Rumbi does, but then they get over it quickly. I would never tell them, but I am so freaking happy to see them. They can be so random, and even though I call them by their Christian names, I do love them. It takes us close to forty minutes to reach the homestead, and I realize that we might have spent the day wandering around again and never making it back, had we not been rescued. How could we have been so blue-eyed. Not much better than zoo-educated Sven.

❖ ❖ ❖

Cousin seems to be the official welcoming committee. She comes out of the granary with an empty sack and hurls herself in our direction, ululating. "Amai," she says, "it is John! Welcome Samaita, welcome! Oh it is you, little mother, who brought them. Amai, you spoke true when you said the day would not end before visitors arrived. Here they are."

She throws herself in a strange not-quite-a-hug, holding onto John's arms and then does the same with Rumbi.

Then she comes to me and grabs my hand, saying, "Ah! Little mother, we thought that maybe you had decided to spend the night in Saratoga. We were wondering what had happened to you. If you had asked me, I would have told you not to go with VaTombo and his crazy donkeys, he is very unreliable."

But she saw us leaving, and she even said goodbye. I just shake my head. Random.

Vimbiko is walking into the clearing from God knows where he disappears to everyday. He wasn't there yesterday when we left. Fiso as usual is by his side.

I'm hoping he doesn't guess that we tried to run away. He looks at us where we are standing, by John's Land Cruiser, and nods his head. By this time my parents have ducked into the kitchen to greet Tete Victoria. The kids are back and the snotty one is pulling on my sarong and asking where I went. I'm not in the mood to play with them, so I head for where Vimbiko is standing, outside the kitchen, but Cousin intercepts me.

She calls me "little mother," amainini, because of who my father is to her in the grand scheme of things. It all made sense in the olden days when everyone lived together in the villages. Nowadays, especially when you don't see half of your relatives most of the time, you hardly know who is who and how they are related to you. So me, I just call everyone "Cousin"—but there's no word for "cousin" in Shona.

"Your Tete wants you to cook the chicken she has killed in honour of your father's visit."

"What! Me, cook a chicken on the fire?"

"Yes, she would like to see how good a cook you are," Cousin says and laughs at the horror on my face. "I don't have time to do that today, I have to go and clean the goat tripe for the feast tonight. Here." She thrusts a metal dish with a headless chicken in my hands.

"You will have to light the fire in the kitchen too. The wood is stacked behind the granary."

With these instructions, she bustles away.

I am quite literally gobsmacked. Me, cook a chicken, on the fire—never mind that I have to light the fire in the kitchen. Maybe I can get Rumbi to do it. I turn towards the kitchen with every intention of somehow getting my mother to do it, when I bump into her right there.

"You're going to cook, Chanda? I'm looking forward to it. I'm sure you'll do a good job and not shame me in front of Tete." And just like that she goes to join Cousin at a small table by the tap, where there are two big dishes, one gleaming with greenish goat guts and the other empty. Rumbi is already in daughter-in-law mode, with her wraparound and her hair tucked away in a scarf like mine and Cousin's. She doesn't even look back.

Swagga and Jix think it's hilarious but make themselves scarce in case they too are given something to do. Sven comes over and takes the dish from me. "At least they have removed the feathers and the insides. It won't be so difficult."

"Oh yeah, like you know! Do you want to give it a shot?"

"I would, but how I see it, you are supposed to do it."

I grab the dish from him and tell him, "I would really appreciate help with the firewood." I give him my nicest smile, even though actually I'm annoyed. I didn't come here to cook. I came here to straighten my memory and get the damn zebra out of my life. Instead I have seen a whole herd! I whirl around and stomp to the kitchen, Sven following. Baba is still in there, talking to Tete Victoria, who is speaking her mind as usual, asking my father why—with such large feet—he cannot see his way to using them on the road to see his relatives. She is telling him that they used to spend days on the road to visit family, because staying connected to each other is important. We are bound by more than just obligations.

Hahaaaa! John is getting a lecture. Serves him right, he is always lecturing me, Mama, and everybody else. Good for him to get some of his own medicine.

When Sven tries to light the fire for me, Tete Victoria tells him to leave women's work to women and go outside to be with the other men. He doesn't understand and I'm glad for that. But he gets the gist by her tone and gives me a look that says "Sorry," and backs out.

I mouth "Thank you."

Vimbiko, seated next to John on the ledge against the

inside wall of the hut, gives me an encouraging smile but remains silent.

John says, "Chanda, are you really going to light a fire and cook? When have you ever done such a thing?"

Yeah, whatever, it's not like I have a choice. And it's not that you ever taught me to do it. What do you expect then?

"You will succeed I'm sure," he says, when he senses that I have not appreciated his no-show of support, "you are ever determined. Just like your name says, whatever you set out to do, you persevere in it."

He gives me a pat on the back, gets up, and stoops to exit. Vimbiko follows him and I am left with Tete Victoria, who is into her snuff again, mumbling under her breath.

What follows promises to be the most miserable cooking hours of my life. Stuck in the dim kitchen with a dead bird, a smoky fire, and a crotchety snuff-taking old woman who has something to say about every move I make and killing herself with husky laughter at my attempts to cut up the chicken, I have never been so close to throwing a fit. Yes, I act out occasionally and indulge in sulks and minor tantrums, but this time I feel like letting loose in a pot-throwing, fire-stomping, weave-tearing hissy fit. I have been drugged and laughed at, have spent a night in a tree after wandering around the bush all day, afraid of local wildlife and waiting for a no-show Vimbiko to rescue us. I haven't had a proper bath in days, and the last of my nails is being remoulded by the heat of the fire. I have really had it, but the one thing that keeps my temper at bay is the very sure understanding that Tete Victoria will not stand for it. So I get on with it.

My chicken is far from fancy, there's no onion or black pepper to throw in the pot. It's basically chicken, cooking fat, salt, and tomatoes, and it tastes delicious when I finally try a small piece.

I sit back on my heels—my knees are long past dead from kneeling over the pot on the iron stand over the firepit—and I wipe my sweaty, sooty face and watering eyes. I feel like I have been at it for days but I can't help it, I smile. I did it!

Tete Victoria sounds unimpressed. "So what am I supposed to eat the meat with? Where are the sadza and the vegetables?"

Ag, you know! So much I could say right now, but why bother, I don't even huff and sigh and bring on the slightest dramatics. I'm beat. I have never cooked the millet sadza they like to eat around here—it looks like chocolate pudding and tastes nothing like it, all grainy and bland; and as for the greens, well, she's going to get what she gets and that's that.

I ask her where the millet meal is, and I send one of the little kids to go and get vegetables. The girl goes without delay. I kind of like that.

The kids here are easy to send around. They don't backchat and they go running wherever you send them. They love having something to do. While I am waiting, I ask Tete Victoria what the feast tonight is all about.

"It is to celebrate the new irrigation system that Vimbiko has engineered."

"Vimbiko . . . engineered . . . something?" I'm stunned.

"Yes. He is a very clever boy. He cares about his roots

and he is always trying to find ways to improve things. We cannot always depend on the rains, you know. Ah, but what would you know about these kinds of things? You city people, growing flowers and lawns and wasting time and money taking care of them. What will you do when you no longer have money for food—eat flowers ehiye-e?" She cackles.

After a while she complains, "I am too old to be waiting this long for my sadza. What is taking you so long? I will be on my way to my maker before you are done. Hayiwha-a!"

"The sadza is boiling."

And the vegetables, thankfully, arrive just then, washed and chopped—thanks to whoever's out there by the tap. I can only imagine it must be Mama. By the time I am released from my ordeal, my eyes have given up watering and they find the sun far too bright. Under Tete Victoria's instructions, I've dished up and fed not only us two, but also some of the people who are outside, mostly the men. I don't know what Mama and Cousin ate. The little kids came to and fro, carrying the plates out to people as instructed by Tete.

Like that, I cooked lunch for the first time in my grand-mother's kitchen. I feel a great sense of achievement, which I can't compare to anything in Harare, and that feeling grows to almost unmanageable proportions when Tete Victoria starts to thank me formally, cupping her palms together and clapping.

"Well done and thank you, Zebra, the special one of chief Mutasa, Tembo, the one to whom praises belong, the white-skinned one, who is to be carried around in honour, the seller of fine linen, the King's special and favourite one. Well done, Dube, the striped one, my dearest Zebra, thank you, the one close to my heart. When you admire a zebra, pay attention to the legs—if you pay attention to the skin you will forget yourself. Well done you of Chikanga, Zebra, the sleek one. Thank you lion of the land, well done indeed, Tembo."

Wow! It's deep. That's the whole history of my clan right there—where they came from, who they were, what they were known for, the various names they have been called over time. This is my family. This feels like coming home, and I wish for a moment that I could have been cooking for my grandmother—my father's mother. I loved her and I have happy memories of her. Tete Victoria is my grandfather's sister and only related to my grandmother through marriage and they are nothing alike.

While I was slogging away in the kitchen, there had been some major cooking going on outside in big black cauldrons on several fires under a corrugated-steel, open-sided shed that seems to have been erected that morning. Mama, Cousin, and some other women were stirring pots of sadza, goat stew, tripe, and vegetables. Turns out people had been fed steadily all day.

It's now sunset and still quite hot outside. Other people from around the area are wandering into the compound and finding places to sit and eat and catch up. They are talking about the lion. It has become very bold, taking a man right outside his hut as he was about to step in after a day at the fields. His wife witnessed the whole thing. It is not safe to walk about, even in your own yard. I wonder at this, since people are busy meandering to and from their homes.

It can't be that bad. The attack must have happened far from here.

"And yet, we cannot just hide in our homes," a man says. "Life continues by the grace of God. You cannot say if I do this or don't do this, I will survive. You survive because God wills it. If it is to die in the mouth of a lion, so be it. It is not as if we have gone looking to be eaten. If a lion wants to eat, it will hunt. If a lion hunts you, you will be eaten. End of story. So let us eat and drink and enjoy life while we still have it."

I'd rather hide and not get eaten. That's my take on that philosophy.

Rumbi gives me a little hug and says, "You cooked a good meal for your Tete. I am proud of you."

John calls me over to where he has one arm around Vimbiko.

"Can you imagine, Chanda? This young man, he is the son of my best friend. His father and I went to school together, and during the holidays we used to get up to mischief here in the village when we came to visit, and now here he is, a model citizen, doing excellent community projects. We need more young men like him around."

John obviously has had a few sips of the Seven Days Brew. He is only this happy and loud when he's a little plastered. It doesn't take much, he doesn't have a good head for alcohol. Even I could drink him under the table.

Vimbiko is laughing along with John. They seem very happy in each other's company. John pats him heavily on the back.

"I look at him and I see my friend when he was young,

when I was young." He gives Vimbiko a big hug.

Eish, John is so on a level right now. This is not the person he is when he's at home. It must be all the fresh air.

Vimbiko laughs and hugs him back, saying, "I will let him know."

"Greetings, yes, and you can give him my number," my father says and pulls a business card out of his wallet.

Vimbiko winks at me and leads John away in the direction of a group of men by the veranda of the brick house. I'm expecting him to come back and talk to me, but—silly me—he moves off to a group of young men under the tree behind the kitchen. I feel like a spare, standing there not sure what to do next. I don't want to go and join Rumbi and Cousin, because only more hard labour lies that way, so I'm relieved to hear Swagga's loud guffaw from the direction of Jix's car. I head that way.

"Yo, Chanda, the domestic goddess. We had some of your chicken, it was dope."

Swagga pulls me into him with one arm. I carefully slither out of his grip. He's leaning on the hood of the car, and Jix and Sven are propped up against a large rock facing him. I'm hit by the strong yeasty smell of the Seven Days Brew that they're sharing from a clay pot. Apparently that's the best way to drink it—sharing it with your friends.

I say, "Hopefully you guys don't backwash."

"It adds to the flavour," Jix replies.

"Sies man! That's just disgusting."

"Come Chanda, drink with us. You're always saying you're one of the guys, so prove it. This stuff is actually quite all right."

I've never liked the taste of beer and I'm not about to start by going hardcore with the traditional stuff.

"With all this stuff in it, like the grain and everything, it must also be quite healthy for you, no?" Sven asks.

Swagga gestures, saying, "There you go! The expert is talking. He is German, they invented beer!"

Jix adds, "Oans, looks like we had our own home brew also for a couple of centuries, and let me tell you, this is the life. You know there's a lion out chowing oans and yet you can still just have a bender like this, where you can eat delicious organic food cooked on an open fire and watch the stars chilling up above. It's a crazy beautiful life, man!" He shouts out the last bit, arms stretched wide to the sky.

It's too early for the guys to be dorped like this, and when Swagga pulls me into his arms and tries to kiss me, I know it's time to go do something else.

He follows me. "Hey! Hey!"

I stop. "Yes."

"What is going on?"

"Don't you see?"

"What?"

"I . . . don't know."

"What?"

"I don't know about many things, anymore."

Now it dawns on him, I can see it in his face. "About us?"

"As well."

"What is this? You don't want to kiss me since we came here, even if I touch . . . "

"And I can't tell you why, because I don't know."

"Just like that?"

"I wish I knew, really, Swagga, life would be easier."

"Hmh."

"I have so much going on, right now, with myself, maybe at the moment it is just too much."

"Too much? With too much you mean me, I'm too much?"

"Not like that."

"Sounds just like that."

"I'm sorry. I can't help it."

He is quiet.

I feel sorry for him, so I tell him, "It's just difficult right now."

"I understand, I understand." With that he turns around and darts back to the boys and the beer.

I'm standing there, empty like the Chinese vase in our hallway and super relieved, when Vimbiko comes and asks me, "You want to go and fetch my drum with me?"

"I heard that!" Swagga yells. "This is a new one. Come with me to fetch my drum!"

Sven wiggles his brows up and down. "Come and fetch my drum eh?" He makes a really sad face.

Jix bursts out laughing.

I am deeply annoyed with these guys. They are being childish. It's a good thing Vimbiko doesn't understand the lingo. He just smiles and holds out his hand. I have to say, I'm feeling very shy to reach out and take it, but I make myself do it just to irritate Swagga. Thankfully, as soon as we walk away, Vimbiko lets my hand go. "I had a feeling Seven Days wouldn't be your thing. Your friends have been at it for some time now. I saved you some of the drink Amai Roddy makes for me with the millet."

He leads me to where he had just been with other young people. Some of them are apparently my cousins, and they are friendly and welcome me into their group. They are speaking to each other in Shona and laughing about something that happened earlier, when they were in the fields helping Vimbiko launch his engineering project. It seems all the action took place while we were making our way back to the homestead.

"If you're still here tomorrow afternoon, maybe we can go down to the fields and I can show you," Vimbiko says.

I say "okay" and accept a tin cup from one of the girls. It's maheu and I like it. It's thick, cold, and sweet and reminds me of Tete Frasia, who used to make it for me when I was little.

A guy goes to get the drums and brings one to Vimbiko. "Here we go, young boy. Fire up, and let's see who is the best drummer this time around. You outlasted me before, this time I'm ready to take you on."

There is a chorus of opinions and encouragements.

Vimbiko smiles, hoists the big drum onto his shoulder, and says, "Come on, old man. I will show you today what it means to beat a drum."

They heat up the skins of the drums by the outside cooking fire not far from the kitchen, and it's a memorable sight: the flickering lights, their glowing faces, eyes alive with excitement and the anticipation of competition. Then we go over to the clearing where the big tree stands. Some old men are sitting there by another small fire and lights have been hung in the tree using a car battery or something. The drumming contest starts.

As the young men beat their drums, people join in and sing. Some young men start to dance. Soon it turns into a dancing competition, and then the drummers begin to compete. Vimbiko takes off his T-shirt, and I have to say, I gave more than a second look. He is built. He looks over at me with a smile as his hands pound furiously to the music, almost as if he's in a trance, losing himself and finding himself there in the beat. He's having the time of his life. I think about Swagga and Jix and their crew, the kind of fun that we have when we're out. It's nothing like this, nothing that actually requires us to show ourselves other than how cool we are and how much we can floss with what we have.

The young women join in the dancing and at one point someone tries to pull me in. There's no way that's going to happen. Normally I would have my vidcam, but I'm not feeling like it right now, it's not the time. Sven decides to join in and I won't even tell you what he looked like, staggering about and trying to dance like everyone else. He even dances with a Schwarzenegger accent. Everyone seems to enjoy his attempts, even encouraging him. I laugh even harder when I think of how badly he's going to be hanging tomorrow.

People are still enjoying the party when Baba, Mama, and I leave. Rumbi and John are given my room, and thus my bed—good luck to them. I sleep on Cousin's thin mattress on her floor, with the kids' little butts pressing into me on both sides. It's not the best, but it's better than the lumpy bed, and surrounded by the kids, I don't even mind the pitch-black of the night. Cousin shares Tete Victoria's mat.

I fall asleep to the sound of drums and voices and laughing and singing.

NO, I WANT TO STAY

I thought Vimbiko and I would be the only ones up, seeing how much everyone got dorped last night—some peeps didn't even sleep—but when I wake up, I am the last person left in the room. Outside is already a hive of activity. Mama is busy washing things at the table by the tap, Cousin is sweeping the clearing with a long grass broom, and people are generally milling about getting the day started. Smoke from the thatched kitchen billows over the huts and a fire is going outside under the open shed with big tins of water on the boil.

Vimbiko finds me when I'm ready for the day and says good morning politely, in his proper Shona, and even though I still find it difficult to speak to him like that, I reply in kind. As usual he is wearing a T-shirt, this one with a faded Snoopy on the front doing a happy dance, and it's quite snug across his chest. If he was at school in Harare he would be a rugby player very much in demand.

"Would you like to come and see my community project now?" he asks.

Quite a pick-up line. "Okay," I say. "Let me get my camera. I'd like to get some footage, if you don't mind. I'm trying to put together something for a film school application."

"It's cool," he says.

On the way there, following a meandering footpath, I ask him, "How come you're staying with my rellies here?"

"After my grandparents passed on, our homestead was left to my uncle, who sold it without anyone knowing, because almost all his relatives now live in different parts of the country. I chose to come and do this project here, because community is what counts, and community development is my thing. My dad also has a connection to your people, being your father's childhood friend."

"What about him, where is he?"

"He is working in South Africa."

The little kids join us, skipping along here and there and everywhere the whole time.

"And your mother?" I ask.

"I live with my mother. My parents are not together anymore."

I should probably find out more, but I'm not sure about asking. I want to know what his father is doing in SA. There are lots of Zimbos working there, many are in good jobs in managerial positions and even more are in service. I wonder where his father falls. If I'm judging a book by its cover, I would say service. A part of me doesn't want my assumption confirmed.

So maybe he's different from the rest of us, but I can't help liking him. There's something really calm and collected about him. He's got this inner confidence that makes him always smile at everyone, and he doesn't seem to care what we think of him. He's really steady and that's nice.

There's a beautiful mist still hovering just above the fields and I capture it on camera. When I cross my index finger over my lips as a sign, the kids are quiet and cover their mouths with both hands. The birds give me a nice backing track with their twittering from the trees. It's all orderly and nicely laid out and green where we are. As soon I stop filming, the kids scream and laugh and yell, they just cannot be still. They want me to record them. The other day I shot them dancing to some local tune they seem to love, and after hearing it about a thousand times, I know the words and actually find myself humming it. But the kids can move! I've got to give them props. When my film is done, it will be so much fun. I don't know what I'll call it, though.

"Chanda?" Vimbiko is waving at me. "I was talking to you."

"Sorry, I was miles away."

He takes me by the arm and points to a structure. It looks like somebody turned a bunch of gigantic Ziploc bags upside down, high as a house. I count twelve in total, three rows of four, waving back and forth as if they were alive, a species from a distant planet ready to conquer earth.

Vimbiko says, "They are made out of big plastic bags sealed together. The morning dew collects inside, and during the day it filters out the moisture. It all runs down the walls into a main hose connected to a solar-powered pump, which drives the water through a system of underground hoses half a metre below the ground, directly to the crops in the fields."

I am in awe. Vimbiko, the future Nobel Prize-winning Zimbabwean.

◆ ◆ ◆

We return to the homestead in time for me to answer a summons to Tete Victoria's "consultation room." I hope she's not going to drug me with that vapour of hers again. I'm surprised when my eyes adjust to the darkness inside the hut and I see Rumbi seated on the cowhide next to John. The atmosphere strikes me as tense. Tete shows me a place to sit on the other side of her. She takes a pinch of snuff up her nostrils before she starts.

"John, son of my brother Jonasi Matibaya. You have been summoned here by your elders through your daughter Chandagwinyira. When Matibaya passed on into the hands of our forebearers, you accepted the leadership of your family and then proceeded to cut ties with your family. This is problematic. You accepted not only the status but all the obligations that go with it and you have not honoured any of these in the past few years. However, this is a topic for the family meeting that will be held following this. Your daughter here, Chandagwinyira, our dear grandmother," she gestures to me, "there is nothing that ails her that cannot be fixed. We here know what it means when the things that happen happen. This name that you gave your child is a family name that has a history behind it. You must consult us who know these things before giving your children these names. It is not a simple thing to speak a word into the life of your child, if you do not know what it brings. You have chosen to leave the family, but you want to keep leadership; you have renounced familial ties, but you give your children family names. You cannot be here and there at the same time. Choose, and choose wisely, but remember, a shadow does not fall where there is no light, nothing is absolute."

She pauses to take some more snuff.

Eish, I don't quite understand what she is saying even though I get the words—but what has she actually said? Choose one or the other, but nothing is absolute? And what is the story behind my name? I want to ask, but I have learnt that it is not wise to just speak up at any odd time when you're in the presence of these oldies. They will shut you down onetime.

Now she is gesturing impatiently for me to bring my hand to her. When I do so, she wraps a bracelet of some kind around my wrist. It is made of three smooth seeds strung through a strip of plaited bark. I must wear it for one full cycle of the moon, she instructs me, and then she gives me another gourd of bitter water to drink.

I'm expecting John and Rumbi to say something in protest, but to my surprise they remain silent. I don't know if I believe what Tete Victoria is saying, but here I am accepting her medicine; this must mean something. Apart from the night spent up the tree, I have not had visions of the zebra since I arrived, and no black spots in my memory. Despite the discomfort of the conditions, I am actually beginning to enjoy being here. It's different and challenging. I don't have to look out for stuff to do to get a kick out of life. Here the kicks come to you. I'm discovering that I like being challenged. I mean, which of my city friends can say they spent a night in a tree fearful of a bunch of lions?

I come to and Tete is now talking to Rumbi and John.

"And why have you, Rumbi, had only one child? What is wrong with your womb that you cannot have more? I can help you if you have those kinds of problems. Or is it John? Are you too busy in your fancy office to come home still fit enough to make children with your wife? Are you experiencing male problems?"

Ha! Tete is on a level. I lean back and feel a little sorry for my parents. Rumbi and John look like they want to evaporate.

"You! You can go now." She means me.

Eish, this old lady is something else, but I am glad she has spared me whatever is coming. I get up and leave Rumbi and John to their fate.

◆◆◆

The guys are in their usual place, on the rocks outside the kitchen. Looks like they intend to become part of the rocks. Swagga squints through his sunglasses and drops his head into his hands. Sven tries to smile and Jix looks like he's ready to drop and stay down. Tea cups lie scattered on the ground; obviously after all the beer they've had, the tea hasn't helped them get back into shape.

I like the tea they make here. Cousin throws everything into a big teapot—water, milk, sugar, and tea leaves—and then it simmers and simmers until it's all thick and delicious and really hot. I decide to go and get some more tea for myself before I deal with these corpses.

I take the empty cups back into the kitchen and return with my second cup of tea and start telling them about Vimbiko's project. They're dying to tell me to shut up but they don't have the strength to say a word. I cheerfully sip my tea and eat my thick slice of bread and jam. The little kids come back again. I don't know how they do it, they are dusty and snotty already, and it's not even noon yet. Every morning they seem to get a big washing, looking fresh and all, but by noon they're rummaging around like a bunch of dirt bike trolls. They bug me to film them again.

"Film us talking, this time. We want to tell your friends in Harare our names and what grades we're in."

"I want to sing my song."

"Eish! Chanda, take your crèche and go far from us. Please," Swagga speaks out from between his knees.

I will be merciful, St Chanda will give the Seven Days Brew adventurers some peace. So I tell the kids, "Okay, let's go over there by the tree," and they follow me, clapping their hands, singing and dancing. They can be really funny, everything sparks them and they're not afraid of much. They keep trying to scare each other, saying the lion will come for this or that one, but they don't seem to be really worried about it.

There's been no news about the lions, and I hope it's one of those cases where they just disappear. Wishful thinking. I don't know much about life in the bush, but I do know that once wild animals start interfering with people, something decisive needs to be done. Vimbiko is hanging out under the big tree. I'm surprised when he asks me why I haven't filmed him yet. I filmed Cousin Amai Roddy and some of the other cousins—Tete Victoria refused—and I have filmed the kids and the fog over the valley, but not him.

Actually, I have been too shy to ask him, and it's great that he's asked me himself. So I say, "Okay, cool."

The little kids are laughing and pulling his hand, asking him if they can be in the film with him. He convinces them to sit quietly and let him do his own film, because they have had their turns.

"Okay," I tell Vimbiko, "speak. Say something." I angle for a head shot.

First off, he smiles and touches his chin lightly, self-consciously. Then he says, in crystal-clear English, "So, my full name is Vimbiko Matidavira Rusike. I come from Gumindoga village, my people are Shava, the Great Eland Bull, those of Guruswa, the ones who carry heavy loads, hunted only by those who do so without caution. My father is an engineering consultant in Johannesburg. I think that is where I got my love for creating things that work and are of use to communities to better their lives. I believe in keeping it real. Even though I live in Harare and attend a Group A school, I prefer to spend my holidays here speaking my mother tongue and increasing my knowledge of where I come from. I am interested in the origins of things because they go a long way in explaining the present and predicting the future. They say history repeats itself, so it is a wise man who knows his history."

I'm speechless. My jaw almost falls off when Vimbiko starts speaking in English, without even a gwash accent. There is no trace of his good Shona in his voice. He displays a bit of attitude, even. It's like the Vimbiko I have known has been taken over by aliens.

When he has finished, I stop recording and stare at him. I

feel foolish and angry at the same time. It seems I'm not the only one who is annoyed—the little kids are complaining that they didn't like his speech, because they didn't understand what he was saying. One of them says he should have let her sing.

"Chanda?"

"Yes."

"You all right?"

"Sure." I have no words right now. How he must have been laughing at us. We are such judgmental idiots, we took one look at him and decided who he was; of course, with a little help from him.

"Why didn't you just say who you really were from the beginning?"

"I did," he replies with a shrug.

"No, you acted like this rural guy who didn't know English and didn't understand what we were saying."

"I never acted. I simply chose to speak in my original language, because that is the language everyone uses around here. You are the ones who kept speaking the way you speak in your homes in town, regardless of the fact that people here wouldn't understand what you were saying to each other."

"We were just being ourselves."

"As was I. This is who I am, when I am here. I don't call people 'dude' and 'bruh' and stand around making fun of people because they live a different life to mine."

"And I don't think that I am so good and special that I am better than everyone just because they don't speak perfect Shona or because they are out of their element. So what if we don't always get it right? That's who I am!"

He is looking at me with his big eyes. After an eternity he says, "I guess it's a tie. Peace?"

I think about it for a minute and decide on the easy option.

"Peace." We shake hands.

"You want to go for a walk?" I ask.

"Sounds good to me."

◆◆◆

First we walk side by side, then he is in front of me when the path narrows to a mere trace through the high grass. The ends touch and we are basically swimming through the field, our arms creating space for our bodies before the golden flood closes in behind us. The bending grass produces a brittle, swishing sound, and grasshoppers and other insects flee in panic, jumping off the ground and whirring off the leaves. I enjoy the silence between us, the fact that he seems to know where he's going and therefore calls the shots and I don't have to make any decisions. Maybe he has a nice place on his mind, a surprise, a nice view.

After about half an hour we stop at a muhute, not too much higher than we are, and Vimbiko carefully pulls off a handful of the dark purple fruit. I like waterberries, even though their texture is a bit weird. When they're ripe and soft like this, they are sweet and the flesh just slips off the seeds. Tete Frasia has a tree in her garden, and when the fruit falls on its own, the purplish-red flesh stains her driveway. We keep walking until, on our left, a wall of brown rock grows straight out of the earth, towering higher than a townhouse in Harare. Its shade invites us to stay longer and we linger. We sit down on the dead trunk of a large tree and the wood creaks under our weight.

"I have to tell you something . . . ," I start.

"What?"

"I forget stuff."

"So do I."

"No, I mean . . . like . . . I am sick."

"How sick? What do you forget?"

"Anything—can be small stuff, could be what I did yesterday morning."

"We all forget . . . "

"No, serious, it is worse with me."

"We are all different."

"I am sick."

"Everybody is . . . "

"Vimbiko."

"Doctor talk."

"But . . . okay . . . now . . . I see . . . things that are not there, I see . . . a zebra."

He looks at me as if somebody wrote a message on my face. "If you close your eyes . . . is it gone then?"

"Yes."

He gives a nod. "Only because a blind man can't see it, that doesn't mean the world doesn't exist. It does."

"So?"

"Maybe most people are just blind to the zebra."

"But I can't touch it. It's not there!"

"You can't touch love either. But it is there."

"That's a feeling."

He shrugs.

How did he get the love idea? Why would he go there so fast? Does he . . . like me? Before I can make a decision, my mouth opens. "Love?"

Suddenly we see bushes stirring and the tall grass waving at us without the slightest sign of a wind. I'm thinking, for once, this is a good moment for my zebra to appear. Maybe Vimbiko could be the first one besides me to see it. The thought disappears when I hear a low growl. I freeze. This could only mean one thing. Please, no! A truck-length in front of us, towards the left, on the path we came on. Its pace is deliberate and slow through the grass. The trees around us are distant and too small to climb, the wall of rock behind us too steep. In front of us, the lioness. We are trapped. The icy coldness of primal fear and looming bloody death creeps up my legs, into my stomach, my chest, and my throat.

And there she is. I see a tawny head partially hidden by the grass. The lioness is still, like she is assessing the situation and making a plan. I don't dare let out a breath. Not a sound is heard anywhere, it's like all the other animals and insects are breathlessly awaiting the coming spectacle. I have nothing on me to fight with, not that a pocket knife or pepper spray would help, and my eyes can't find anything lying around. Vimbiko hasn't even brought his cane. His hand finds mine, and I squeeze so hard I'm surprised I don't hear bones cracking.

"What now?" I whisper.

"Nothing," he says.

"What do you mean nothing?"

"We sit and stay as still as possible."

"We have to . . . run . . . fight . . . make a plan, something . . . "

"Shhh, there is no way out. We have to face her."

"How can you . . . You want to give up?"

"I don't give up. I just . . . accept."

"Accept what?"

"Fate, destiny."

The grass moves again and for a brief moment we see her sandy brown flank between the golden stalks.

We are so dead. When will they find us? What will they find of us? Both of us? No. The lion will grab one of us and drag him or me into the bushes. Whom will she take? Probably me, with my big juicy thighs. Maybe Vimbiko will fight for me, tear her apart with his bare fists, tackle her before she can sink her teeth into me. Maybe she'll take him instead, he has muscular thighs and is beefier overall. He'd make a much better meal than me, I'm sure. What then? Would I try to save him? I bet the lioness grabs me because I'm the smaller prey and Vimbiko will make like Usain Bolt and gap it. He'll get back to the compound and shrug and say, "That's the way the dice fell."

"Why did we come here in the first place?"

"You wanted to go for a walk."

This guy is not for real. Branches crack and we see the shoulder between the bushes, she sits down, still observing us.

"Why is she getting comfortable?" I whisper through the side of my mouth. "Maybe she's waiting for the rest of her homies."

"Maybe she's not hungry and isn't bothered with us."

I feel sick, my knees are made of sadza.

"I am dying today. I'm so dead."

"If it is your time—"

"Shut up with that! Just shut up. I don't want to die like that, getting—"

"Shhh, you are too loud, your voice, keep it down."

"Maybe that will do it, we yell at her, be loud! That could chase her away."

"Have you ever heard that yelling helps against a lion?"

"I don't know."

"I wouldn't chance it."

Where is my zebra? Where are the zebras that helped me and my friends the other night, protected us?

I mimic his voice: "If it is your time, it is your time." No reaction from his side. "You are young, educated, an engineer, good-looking, soon a—"

"Thank you." He casts me a smile with one corner of his mouth.

"Wh . . . You're welcome." I'm blushing.

"I like your eyes."

He looks at me. The lion looks at me. Both sort of hungry. Flirting during dinner is cool—if you are not the dinner!

The cracking of dry wood makes us lose eye contact without moving heads. Out of the corner of my eye I see the lioness leaving the bushes, coming directly towards us, looking neither left nor right, and she's not trying to be quiet or cautious anymore. She is sinking lower and lower into a crouch as she moves towards us. She's done making a plan. It's time for execution.

I'm shaking, rattling actually, holding Vimbiko's hand. I

love my life, I love it, I love how I am, with my thick thighs, messed-up weave, and memory glitches. I love my life, my parents, my family, I love him, Vimbiko—okay, I have strong feelings.

She is close and fully crouched, ready to pounce. A heat wave travels through my body and I break into a sweat all over. This is it. I open my mouth to scream but nothing comes out, tears are streaming down my cheeks. I turn to Vimbiko and we press our lips together for our first and last kiss, salty with my tears and . . . A shot rings out, so loud, I shoot up like a rocket, standing straight beside Vimbiko. It's like I'm tumbling around inside my head and nothing is the right way up. What happened? I squeeze my eyes shut and take a deep breath. When I open them, I see the lioness sideways on the ground, close to my feet, her legs jerking, milky eye staring dead at me while dark blood pulsates from the wound in her lifeless body.

◆ ◆ ◆

The Rangers drive us back to the compound with the body of the old lioness in the back of their open Land Rover. They congratulate us on keeping cool and staying still. We made their clear shot possible—as involuntary live bait.

This morning they had rounded up the younger lions of the pride and concentrated on the lioness. It was perfect timing. The level of excitement at our arrival in the village is straight-up ballistic. First there is much weeping and wailing at the thought of our almost certain death. The men generally grunt and shake their heads and make extended sounds of disbelief—"Mai-wehhhh! Mai-wehhhh!"

punctuated with "Oh those children were dead today! They were dead! Surely so dead. Dead as dead as can be."

We have to tell the story over and over, and each time I calm down a little bit more. Mama almost passes out and she and John hug me forever, and we are passed around as everyone else grabs us in turn, squeezing us and jumping up and down like crazy pistons, jarring everything in my body. Cousin Amai Roddy, Tete, and the other women are ululating and singing that the Creator is good. For some reason, they sing Vimbiko's praises because, of course, in their minds there is no question that I am returned safe because I was with him.

"Thank you Shava, the Great Animal, he who chases those who portend death, whose tears are too sacred to fall to the ground . . . who is given wives in the country of the Njanja people . . . " and so on. The Great Eland Bull.

Whatever! All he did was tell me to sit still and be quiet and talk about the roll of the dice. I guess in a way his calmness did kind of save us. If I had tried to run, things could have turned out much different.

For the rest of the day there are celebrations and I am fed and petted and hugged and thumped on the back and there is no talk of leaving. Again and again my eyes find Vimbiko's.

◆ ◆ ◆

Next morning after breakfast we plan our trip home. My father and Sven have concluded that our Land Cruiser with its powerful engine can easily tow the Peugeot back to Harare. But as the preparations proceed, I realize that I'm not so sure that I want to leave in such a hurry.

"I'm staying here. Just for a bit."

That's what they were expecting, or maybe hoping not to hear—Swagga, at any rate. He's not impressed. He knows something's up between Vimbiko and I. He turns his head away, and my parents ask, "What are you thinking?"

"I think I'd like to be here for another couple of days." Or weeks. "I don't know. I like it here. I feel better. I haven't seen the zebra, and I think my memory has improved too." And Tete Victoria has said that she will take me to the place where the original Chanda was laid to rest, and tell me the full story. I want to know the story of my name.

I don't need to convince them. Baba says he will send a driver to fetch me when I'm ready to come home, and less than an hour later half of the village waves goodbye as they drive off, my parents in their Land Cruiser and the boys in the squeaking Peugeot in tow. We hugged goodbye, Swagga only shortly, with closed eyes.

I wonder if that car will make it to Harare even towed. Good that there is enough space for the boys in our SUV, if it doesn't. In Harare they will drop Sven at Roadport to catch an overnighter for down South. Swagga and Jix are anxious to fill their Boogie Down Production crew in on all the details of their trip to the countryside, and they will embellish everything to distortion. I bet they will even say they were the ones who faced down the lioness! While Jix is gung-ho about coming back, maybe even moving here for some time, Swagga can only shake his head at the idea. My parents will visit Tete Frasia to tell her all the news they heard from the family—John had to promise this to Tete Victoria.

Cousin is standing to my left and Vimbiko to my right, when he fishes a cellphone out of his pocket and says casually, "I'll be back in a second, I have to make a call."

My jaw drops—an all-too-familiar facial dysfunction lately when I'm around him. "Wh . . . wow, hey, what? Where? How?"

"Up there. Where else?" He points to the red rock on top of the hill.

"What . . . is there?"

"There we get signal."

"Isn't that . . . isn't that where people go . . . deep into . . . into contact with the universe and all?"

"Well, that's our country slang for making a phone call."

"You. Are. Kidding. Me."

We start walking up the hill, the kids behind us.

"No."

"Why didn't you tell me?"

"It wasn't your time."

"What?"

"You didn't ask. Anybody. You guys just tried it everywhere else. Everywhere but there. Seemed to us like you didn't want to go into deep contact with . . . "

"Pah, you saw us and you didn't say anything. Everybody saw us, somebody could've told us. It was pretty obvious what we were doing, wasn't it?"

"Sure. But just because the toddler throws a tantrum, he doesn't get what he wants."

"Toddler? Are you comparing me with a toddler?"

"I am not saying that. You have no phone anyway."

"I had it to a point, then I lost it, before . . . I would've liked to phone somebody, you know. I could've borrowed a phone from . . . you!"

"Yes. You want it now?"

"YES!"

"Okay, I'll give it to you as soon as we are up and have a signal. Who do you want to call?"

"Tete Frasia."

"Ah."

"You know her?"

"She told us you were coming and why and so on."

I walk a few steps in silence. Inside of me a volcano is churning.

He asks, "Are you thirsty? Should we go make our calls and . . . "

"No! You . . . You mean everybody knew . . . knew . . . about my memory, the zebra . . . ?"

"Yes, sure, yes. Calm down."

I don't feel like being calm. I'm so annoyed, but the climb is making me out of breath. We are going up the steep hill over a well-walked path of stone steps to the top. The kids are following us, skipping, chattering, and stopping to pull wild fruits off branches and stuff them into their mouths.

"So that was all hocus-pocus. Everything that Tete did?"

"No."

"It was all a big lie." I am scanning the horizon for our car and the Peugeot. Gone. I'm stuck.

"No!"

"What now? All the deep-based spirituality, the ancestors . . . "

"No, no, no, Chanda, that is true, honest, real, we only

wanted to know what was what before we had to rely on somebody who can't even ask for a place to get a phone signal!"

I stomp my foot.

"Yeah, you have an explanation for everything."

"It's not like that. We just wanted the best result, for everyone. Tete Frasia thought the same when she phoned. No one was sure how long you would stay and the tetes didn't want your time here to be wasted."

I chew on this for a while. I'm not sure how I feel about the way everything happened. I feel a little like everyone made a fool of me. A horrible thought pops into my head.

My teeth grind, and I ask, "Tell me . . . Swagga, Jix and . . . Sven weren't in it as well?"

"No, that's why we had to fill them up so you were on your own."

"Fill them up . . . the Seven Days Brew! That was on purpose?"

"The whole feast was on purpose."

Nothing surprises me anymore.

We finally reach the hilltop with the red rock upon it.

He asks me, "You never been up here?"

I'm sweating, my shirt sticks to my back. "No."

The rock looks like it has a little cubby hole carved into it. Cousin is inside; she pockets her phone and comes out. I notice that the hole even has a smooth shelf to sit on.

He says, "Looks just like a British phone booth without windows, doesn't it?"

Uhhhh? Okay. No it doesn't, but what do I know. I'm the big dum-dum from the city.

Cousin says, "Five bars today. It's all yours."

We thank her and I facepalm myself.

Vimbiko pushes his speed dial.

"Who are you phoning?"

"Tete Frasia."

"You have her on speed dial?"

"You never know." He hands me his phone, a brand I don't know.

"Is this a Samsung, an iPhone, or . . ."

"It's not out yet. It's a prototype, it will hit the market just before Christmas. New competitor for apples, pears, and plums. Made in Iceland. Faster, thinner, lighter, waterproof. To unlock it you need your thumbprint and it comes with a boomerang app. If you throw it like a boomerang it comes back to you."

I must look like a kangaroo in headlights.

"I was kidding . . . with the boomerang thing."

I hear Tete Frasia. "Vimbiko from beautiful Gumindoga."

"No, Chanda from hell!"

"Oh my dear, how are you?"

"I bet you know."

"He told you already? Oh dear . . ."

"Stop dearing me, do you know how I feel?"

"Better, much better, I heard, your cousin just told me."

I cringe and look down the hill after Cousin. "Arrrgh, Tete, why?"

Vimbiko says loudly, "I told her that too."

"I am talking!" My free hand slams against the red phone booth of a rock.

"Yes?" I hear Tete.

"You think this is fair?"

"Life isn't fair, you remember? It's what you make with it. And everybody did their best over the last days, including you."

"So . . ."

"The result counts."

"The result ended up in front of a lion! Do you know that?"

"Yes, of course, but it wasn't your time."

I really have to work hard at calming down. Anyway, my anger bounces off my relatives like a rubber ball. I can twist and turn it all I want, she is right, Vimbiko is right, I am better. That counts. Only that. And they did it because they wanted to help me. The thing is, I probably wouldn't have told them anything. They would've been right about me. I somehow would've hoped to keep it strictly between me and Tete Victoria—well, as few people as possible, but it doesn't seem to work like that out here. Seems everyone is in it together. We're all in it together.

"Dear?"

"Yes?"

"I thought the connection broke off."

"No, the connection was never better."

◆ ◆ ◆

"John."

"Yes, Tete Victoria."

"Don't you know, you cannot just name your children without the advice of your elders."

"But . . . what is it with Chanda's name?"

"Let me tell you . . . The very first Chandagwinyira was a very beautiful and wise woman—a revered healer in her village. She loved and was loved deeply by one of the village herdsman, Tayidei, but the son of a chief from a far-off village named Matibura had heard about her beauty and coveted her. After repeated and unsuccessful attempts to win her favour, he finally led a raid on Chanda's village, burning their stores and destroying their crops, killing all their animals. Chanda fled with Tayidei to a secret place in the hills, but after weeks of suffering under Matibura and his men, someone from the village betrayed Chanda and she was captured while Tayidei was out hunting. En route to the chief's village Chanda learned that it was Tayidei who had given her up to Matibura to save the village. Anger gave her the strength to overcome her guard and escape, but they had travelled for many days and she was unfamiliar with the land and was soon lost. The chief's son had many skilled trackers in his party, and she knew it would only be a matter of time before she was found. One night, she sought shelter in a cave. She could hear Matibura's dogs barking in the distance, and soon they found her. She was tired and outnumbered, the only way to escape was across a fast-flowing river that was known to never allow anyone who entered it the chance to leave. If it came down to that, she thought, she would put herself at the mercy of the river spirits rather than go meekly into a life of gilded slavery and live with Tayidei's betrayal. As she walked out of the cave to face her fate, she heard a voice say to her, 'I will help you.' And before her very eyes stood the totem animal of her father's people—a magnificent zebra, its coat glistening in the gloom. Being accustomed to spiritual things, Chanda was not alarmed, she knew this was her father's people come to save her. 'But once you leave this place, you will forget it and never return.' Chanda wanted more than anything to escape. She was tempted for a moment to give herself up for the chance of revenge against Tayidei, but she simply said, 'I will go.' And this is how Chanda came to Gumindoga. She lived a good life here among people of her father's clan until in her old age she began to remember where she had come from and began to tell the story. From that point, things started to go wrong in the village—crops dying, animals becoming sick, even the weather changed and became unpredictable and hostile. Chandagwinyira knew that by remembering, she had brought with her all the bad things from her past into the village, and she asked for help from her ancestor spirits to help her forget again, but she couldn't just forget the distant past anymore, she was now forgetting even things that had just happened, until she only knew what was happening right then and nothing else. By the time she died, peace had been restored to Gumindoga and all Chanda's memories went with her. Before she crossed over she was supposed to close the door to the forgetting, but of course she could not remember. The name Chanda has been associated with forgetting and every so often, children given that name are afflicted by Chanda's subconscious need to forget. If the name is given, it must always be cleansed first of this affliction. This is why, John, you cannot just name your children without the advice of your elders."

"And? Did you . . . is Chanda . . . cleansed now?"

"What do you think?"

QUESTIONS FOR DISCUSSION

1. How would you describe Chanda? Do you like her as a character? Is it important for you to like the main character in a book?

2. In the beginning of the story, what are Chanda's parents watching on television? Why doesn't Chanda like it?

3. What does the zebra symbolize in this novel? What do *you* associate with the zebra?

4. Explain the significance of the title. Do you have a totem? If not, what would your totem be?

5. Describe the dynamic between Chanda and the people in the village.

6. What message does the novel carry about tradition and identity? How would you describe Chanda and Swagga from this perspective? How would you describe *yourself* from this perspective?

7. Compare and contrast Chanda and Swagga. What do you think about their relationship and how it developed?

8. What do you think of Vimbiko? Compare him with Swagga.

9. Describe Sven's role in the novel. If you were a tourist on a journey like his, what would you have done?

10. Is Chanda "cured" at the end of the novel? Explain your thoughts.

11. Could the novel have been written from another character's point of view? If so, how would you imagine the conclusion?

ACKNOWLEDGEMENTS

The authors thank their families, HALD in Denmark for their Writer's Residency program, the Southern Albertan Ethnic Association, and the Public Library and the University Library of Lethbridge, Alberta, Canada.

Clan praise poetry courtesy of:

Poetry International Zimbabwe article entitled "Shona Praise Poetry" by Mickias T Musiyiwa;

Translation of Chanda's praise poem by Ignatius T Mabasa (with thanks).